IN LOVE AND WAR

IN
LOVE
AND
WAR

Barbara Ker Wilson

THE WORLD PUBLISHING COMPANY

CLEVELAND AND NEW YORK

Published by The World Publishing Company
2231 West 110th Street, Cleveland 2, Ohio

Library of Congress Catalog Card Number: 63-10857

First American edition 1963

Published in England under the title
Last Year's Broken Toys

WP263

Contents

People in the Story

SUZANNE SINCLAIR *a young schoolmistress*

CLOTHILDE DUCHESNE *her aunt*

VERNON SINCLAIR *her father*

ERICH HOFFMAN *a German engineer*

MARY *a domestic servant*

JOHN and MARGARET STANFORD *senior partner of Stanford & Earle, and his wife*

PAULINE and FLORA STANFORD *their daughters*

HENRY and LILY MAWTON *Managing Director of Mawton's Mineral Waters, and his wife*

CLIVE MAWTON *their son*

MARION GRAY *shorthand typist at Stanford & Earle*

EVA *her sister*

MR. & MRS. THOMAS GRAY *parents of Marion and Eva*

KEN MARTIN *Eva's boy friend*

People in the Story

ACKNOWLEDGMENTS

The author gratefully acknowledges the help she has obtained from Katharine Savage's admirably concise book, *The Story of the Second World War* (Oxford University Press), and records her thanks to Mrs. Savage for reading the manuscript of this story for historical accuracy.

She is grateful to the authors and publishers for permission to quote the following extracts from their works: "The Blind," "For Johnny," and "Security" from *Collected Poems* by John Pudney (the author and Putnam & Co., Ltd., London); "The War Films" by Sir Henry Newbolt from *New Paths on Helicon, Part II* (Thomas Nelson & Sons, Ltd.); "The Ballad of London River" by May Byron from *Blackwood's Magazine,* 1903 (William Blackwood & Sons, Ltd.); "We'll Meet Again" (Dash Music Company, Ltd.); "Olga Pulloffski" (Francis, Day & Hunter, Ltd.); "We're Going to Hang Out the Washing on the Siegfried Line," "South of the Border," and "I'm Going to Get Lit Up" (Peter Maurice Music Co., Ltd.).

IN LOVE AND WAR

Peace for Our Time

Crewe station: October, 1938. Slanting, soot-laden autumn sunshine filtered through the glass roof upon family groups returning from late summer holidays; anxious mothers keeping tight hold of the youngest children with sticky handclasps; fathers grasping overloaded suitcases filled with crumpled clothes; boys and girls trailing mackintoshes and rugs. Porters trundled barrows, making their way through the crowd with their ancient cry: "Mind yer backs there!" People with time to spare paused to buy tea in thick white earthenware cups, take cigarette packets or slabs of chocolate from slot machines, or linger by the bookstall, beflagged with multicolored magazines like a pavilion on a battlefield.

A row of this week's *Picture Post* was strung across the bookstall. The cover showed a photograph of Adolf Hitler superimposed upon a Nazi flag bearing the black claw of the Swastika: Adolf Hitler, with the eyes of a fanatic and the toothbrush mustache which, by some freak of fortune, gave his features a first-glance similarity to those of Charlie Chaplin. As if to deprecate this menacing portrait, the headlines of the newspapers on the stall, overlapped upon each other as precisely as Patience cards, carried the reassurance of the Munich message. "Peace for Our Time." "Peace With Honor—P.M." "Chamberlain the Peacemaker." And, further to dispel anxiety about the Dictator of Nazi Germany, whose Storm Troopers were now goose-stepping into the Sudetenland, there were all those other beguiling picture-papers and magazines: *Picture Goer,* with Deanna Durbin's dazzling smile on the cover; *Stitchcraft,* advertising new knitteds for autumn; *Home Chat,* with a special offer of California Poppy perfume; *Illustrated,* showing a colored photograph of the two little Princesses, Elizabeth and Margaret Rose.

An announcement, blurred and crackling, sounded across the station.

"Passengers for Renchester change here and join the train now standing on Platform Five . . ."

Certain Rencastrians regarded the lack of a through train from London to Renchester as an affront to their dignity; from time to time, letters appeared in the *Renchester Echo* upbraiding the London Midland & Scottish Railway. But these were Rencastrians with an overgrown sense of the importance of their provincial town. Renchester was not, after all, so vital a center of commerce and industry as, say, Birmingham, Glasgow, Manchester, or Belfast. The town's main importance lay in the few shipyards clustered round the wide mouth of the river Ren, where some seventeen centuries ago the Romans had built a fortified camp.

Among the travelers who crossed over to Platform

Five on this particular afternoon were a young man and a young woman as yet unknown to one another. By chance they found places in the same compartment of the Renchester train. Because of this, their destinies were to be linked in a way that would have seemed impossibly melodramatic, unbelievably fantastic, even to the most devoted picture-goer among the crowd which thronged the station.

Yet Suzanne Sinclair and Erich Hoffman were only two figures more deeply etched among all those others. All these travelers so eager to complete their journeys that day, to make connections, find empty seats, not lose their tickets, their children, or their luggage, were on the verge of a catastrophe that was to involve them in a common drama of life and death. Unaware of the individual parts they were to play, they sipped tea, smoked cigarettes, hailed taxis, greeted one another, waved good-by, and scanned timetables as though their sole occupation were in the role of "traveler in a railway station."

Three years hence, they would have stared, astonished as travelers from another age, to see the station in wartime, the word CREWE obliterated from every nameboard, the cigarette and chocolate machines empty for the duration, the glass roof shattered, and at night the sky above alive with probing searchlights while gunfire sounded in the distance.

Suzanne hurried across to the Renchester train, thankful to be on the last lap of her return home. She was tired after the Channel crossing and the tedious journey from London. Her dark hair, short and curly, was tinged with bronze in the dusty sunlight. She wore a deep-blue coat and skirt, and looked about nineteen. In fact, she was twenty-two. As she passed the bookstall, she gave the newspaper headlines a brief glance. She had read the news twice already: once in a French newspaper, on her way to Calais in the Paris boat train, and again in the *Daily Mail*.

Was it true that by intervening in the quarrel between Germany and Czechoslovakia, Neville Chamberlain, Britain's Prime Minister, had achieved "peace for our time . . . with honor"? The *Daily Mail* seemed more certain this was so than did the French newspaper Suzanne had read.

In May, following his invasion of Austria, Hitler had massed troops along the border of Czechoslovakia. In the Sudetenland there was a strong Nazi political party that wanted this area of Czechoslovakia to become part of the German Reich, as Austria had recently done. The Czech government was faced by Nazi demands, both from without and within their country, that the Sudetenland should be ceded to Germany. There was every sign that Hitler intended to invade Czechoslovakia if these demands were refused. The Czech army mobilized and prepared to resist attack.

Then, on September 15, in a desperate effort to avert war between Germany and Czechoslovakia, Mr. Chamberlain had flown to see Hitler in his mountain fastness of Berchtesgaden; a week later there was a second meeting at the Rhineland town of Godesberg. On each occasion, Hitler's demands for taking over the Sudetenland grew more obdurate. The British Prime Minister conferred with the French ministers. France at this time had a defense treaty with Czechoslovakia, but felt unable to help the Czechs to defend their frontiers without British support, and this was not forthcoming. Britain and France now told President Beneš of Czechoslovakia that he must either concede the Nazi demands or else face the threat of Nazi invasion alone.

It was at this juncture that Suzanne had made arrangements to visit her Aunt Clothilde during the half-term vacation. Suzanne taught French and German at Renchester High School, her first post on leaving the University. Aunt Clothilde and Suzanne's cousin, Raoul, always teased her about her choice of career, and called her "the English governess." Suzanne's father was dubious about a trip to the Continent in the middle of the political crisis. "If anything happens . . ." he had murmured, with visions of his daughter stranded on the other side of the English Channel. But Suzanne knew how much her aunt, who was widowed, looked forward to her yearly visit. Aunt Clothilde had been very close to Suzanne's mother, her younger sister. She had missed Lenore greatly when she married Vernon Sinclair and went to live in Renchester, which Clothilde thought of as "that dreary English town." She had only visited Renchester twice. The last occasion was her sister's funeral, ten years ago.

In the event, Suzanne was not stranded on the other side of the Channel. She enjoyed her visit to Paris, staying in her aunt's apartment in the Rue de Fleurus, near the Sorbonne. Cousin Raoul, who was eighteen, was a cadet at L'École Militaire. One morning Suzanne and her aunt watched him take part in a parade. Most of all, Suzanne had enjoyed indulging in her favorite pastime of exploring the ancient quarter around the University, strolling by the Seine, and window-shopping in the fashionable streets of the Right Bank.

Meanwhile, President Beneš had reluctantly agreed to concede the Nazi demands, as Britain and France had advised. Mr. Chamberlain flew to Germany a third time, and on September 29 the Munich Conference took place between Hitler, Chamberlain, M. Daladier of France, and Benito Mussolini, Dictator of Italy. Nazi Germany and Fascist Italy had combined to form a military alliance: the Axis. On the last day of September, the Munich Pact was signed—the agreement which recognized German rights in the Sudetenland and virtually handed over the territory. In return, *Hitler promised to make no further territorial claims in Europe.* Yesterday, Mr. Chamberlain had arrived home. Today, the newspapers ran their jubilant banner headlines and showed photographs of the Prime Minister, with his famous umbrella, arriving at Heston airport and waving aloft the paper bearing the agreement signed by Herr Hitler.

And today the arguments and discussions began. Had Britain and France shown strength of purpose as peacemakers? Or had they acted with fatal weakness, giving in to Hitler once again, as they had previously given in to him over the question of large-scale German rearmament and over the Nazi annexation of Austria?

Suzanne had overhead one argument as she drank a cup of coffee at Victoria. Two commercial travelers, tucking into plates of sausages and baked beans, had sat at the table next to hers. One of them was a lean, hatchet-faced man.

"Chamberlain!" he had said scornfully. "What's he

achieved by dashing off to Munich? 'Peace for our time'? Don't you believe it! All he's succeeded in doing is to pacify Hitler for a while by throwing him a slice of someone else's country." He pointed his fork at his companion, half a sausage impaled on the prongs. "You mark my words—there'll be a general European war before we know where we are. I give it another six months . . . nine at the outside."

The other man was plump and jolly-looking, with a mustache that dripped tea when he drank. "Hitler will never take on France and Britain together," he said confidently. "He couldn't do it."

"Couldn't he? What makes you so sure of that?" The thin prophet of doom shoveled baked beans into his mouth. "I only hope the Government will have the sense to build up our armaments now, before Adolf Hitler strikes again. We need airplanes . . . bombs . . . guns . . ."

Bombs . . . guns. . . . Suzanne had felt a spasm of fear. She recalled a remark Aunt Clothilde had made while they watched the parade at L'École Militaire.

"They look very splendid, these young men of ours. Pray God they will not have to fight." Her aunt's eyes had darkened as she turned to Suzanne. "We in France are always more aware of danger than the British on their island. Five times in a hundred years the German guns have been heard in Paris. 'Don't worry,' they say; our army—the French army—is supposed to be the finest in the world; the British navy is said to be invincible. And yet—I am afraid. There is a fanatic leading Nazi Germany today. He will stop at nothing."

As he passed the station bookstall with the photographs

of the *Führer,* Erich Hoffman automatically registered
a "Heil Hitler!" and in imagined action raised his arm
in the Nazi salute. The *Führer* . . . who, since his rise to
power five years ago, had done so much for the Father-
land, restoring Germany to her rightful place as one of
the leading countries of Europe. And before long—the
Führer had promised this—Germany would be the most
powerful nation in the world!

Erich was slight in build, with a Teutonic fairness. He
carried a suitcase in one hand, and in the other a briefcase which contained photographic equipment. On top of
the neatly folded clothes in his suitcase was the little Nazi
flag he carried everywhere, as another might carry the
photograph of a dear relative or friend. Erich had been
presented with the flag when he joined the Hitler Youth
Movement as a schoolboy. His passport was safely lodged
in the breast pocket of his sports coat. ERICH HOFFMAN—
Beruf: Ingenieur. *Geburtsort:* Stuttgart. *Geburtstag:*
24.9.1918. *Wohnort:* Berlin. And tucked inside the front
cover was the leaflet issued with each Nazi passport, "Advice to Travelers Abroad," which carried this message at
the foot of every page: *Gedenke, dass du ein Deutscher
bist!—Remember that you are a German!*

He hurried down the length of the Renchester train,
close behind a slim, dark-haired girl in a deep-blue coat
and skirt.

At last. A compartment with some spare places. Suzanne
opened the door; Erich followed her inside. The people
already seated in the compartment seemed to regard their
entrance with vague hostility; this British trait amused
the French half of Suzanne's nature. Erich, with the

politeness of a stranger, placed her suitcase on the luggage rack for her.

"Excuse, please," he said. "This train will stop at Renchester?"

Suzanne recognized him as a German by his accent and his very correct manner. She almost expected to see him click his heels together as she replied: "Yes. We arrive in three-quarters of an hour."

They sat in two facing seats. Erich produced a technical manual and was soon absorbed in it. Suzanne leaned her head against the prickly third-class moquette and closed her eyes. The other people in the compartment settled down again after the interruption of Crewe and the invasion of this young man and woman. A woman in one corner was knitting with great concentration. Odd to see the British way of knitting again, Suzanne thought, glancing at the clicking needles through half-closed eyes. In another corner sat a large, florid man who might be a commercial traveler. Perhaps there were samples of brushes—or cheap metal cigarette cases or a new line in cleaning fluids—in the fiber suitcase in the rack above his head.

Another corner was occupied by a rosy-cheeked girl wearing a black suit with a pink satin blouse. She looked hot, and her suit was creased and covered in specks of dust. In the patent leather handbag on her lap (though neither Suzanne nor anyone else in the compartment was aware of this) was a packet of sandwiches she had been longing to eat ever since lunchtime. But somehow it seemed too daring a maneuver to produce them. That lady with the knitting would be sure to raise her eyebrows, the gentleman opposite would twitch his nose at the pungent smell of cheese and pickle, and there would be an embarrassing crackle of greaseproof paper. . . . The girl, whose name was Mary, was going into service in Renchester. She hadn't wanted to leave the farm-laborer's cottage where she had lived all her life, but there were no jobs to be had in the country, so there was nothing for it but to go to work in the town.

The scenery between Crewe and Renchester was not beautiful. The train windows framed commonplace views of fields drifting in coils of white smoke from the engine; high embankments studded with telegraph poles; deserted platforms of stations so unimportant as to be called "Halts." Suzanne's eyelids half-opened, drooped, and closed. Suddenly she started as she felt a hand upon her shoulder.

"Excuse—I thought perhaps you wish to be at Renchester. We are arrived."

The young German, on his feet, was smiling diffidently.

Renchester already! Suzanne looked out of the train window. Yes, there was the length of the platform sliding to an illusory standstill, the familiar lines of grimy back-to-back houses huddled alongside the station, the hoardings advertising Mazawattee Tea, Virol for Growing Children, Mawton's Mineral Waters . . .

Suzanne smiled her thanks and got up from her seat. The German handed down her suitcase. Together with the girl in the black suit, they stepped out onto the platform. Erich Hoffman looked around, located the station exit, and walked towards it. Suzanne followed him, seeking her father's face at the ticket barrier, glad to be coming home to the ugly, well-loved house in St.

Oswald's Terrace with her father's brass plate at its door: Vernon Sinclair, M.D.

This brief encounter was all that passed between Erich Hoffman and Suzanne Sinclair that autumn afternoon. Had the young German not possessed such an excellent memory, it might have remained their sole point of contact in life.

Collision

Uptown, downtown; west end, east end: like all provincial towns, Renchester was a patchwork of districts that held both geographical and social significance. "Downtown" denoted the rows of mean little houses by the station, clustered around the gasworks and the mineral water factory, the back lanes between them strung with washing lines. The slums—narrow tenements and streets of once-respectable mid-Victorian houses now overrun by the families of the disreputable (the deprived, the feckless, and the merely unfortunate)—were concentrated in Renchester's east end, a seedy, sleazy area that lay beyond the old Infirmary. Here, shrill-voiced, barefooted children played in the streets, "old women" (some nearly forty) with black shawls drawn over their heads, sat on doorsteps smoking clay pipes, while their men made an occupation of unemployment, dividing their days between futile activities.

"West end" meant the shopping center, where yellow tramcars ground their way along the High Street, and

Burridge's Emporium dominated the skyline. "Uptown" referred to the high ground where All Saints Church and the War Memorial stood, the hills where once Roman sentries had kept watch. Close by were the Memorial Recreation Ground, the High School standing behind spiked iron railings, and St. Oswald's Terrace, where most of the town's surgeons and dentists had their homes.

Dockland lay on the other side of the river, across the wide span of the suspension bridge: steep cobbled streets of red-brick "cottages" led down to the shipyards, and the air was filled with the clamor of hammers on steel and the hoot of sirens.

On the outskirts of Renchester sprawled labyrinthine new housing estates, both council estates which formed part of the town's slum-resettlement scheme, and the cul-de-sacs, crescents, and avenues of bungalows and semi-detached bijou residences built by private speculators.

And then there was Parklands. Parklands, situated near All Saints and the High School, within walking distance of St. Oswald's Terrace, yet an entity within the uptown district. This was Renchester's most exclusive residential address; here lived her wealthiest and most influential citizens, whose wives all held monthly accounts at Burridge's and bought their clothes from the model gown department.

In whichever one of these areas they lived, all Rencastrians shared to a greater or lesser extent the Renchester accent: broadly pronounced vowels and a sing-song intonation of every sentence. Downtown, the accent was really broad, sometimes incomprehensible to a stranger. Uptown, it was often scarcely discernible.

You entered Parklands through high wrought-iron gates opening onto a graveled private road, flanked by horse-chestnut trees. Even the toughest street boys from downtown dared not venture here to raid these trees at conker time. Large, gabled houses, each surrounded by a fenced acre or so of lawns and flower beds, were set back from the road. Most had notices on their gates that said, "No Hawkers or Circulars" and "Tradesmen Side Entrance."

A good many of the downtown dwellers might have seen some irony in the "Tradesmen Side Entrance" direction; most of the Parklands residents had made their money out of trade. Henry Mawton, of Mawton's Mineral Waters, lived here; so did Tobias Clark, proprietor of the town's six-branch grocery business; Percy Harriman, the builder, who had made a fortune out of the new housing estates, and Joseph Paston, who owned the Renchester Model Steam Laundry and underpaid the fourteen-year-old school-leavers who came to work there. Not all, however, were in trade. Professional folk lived here too—the Member of Parliament for Renchester North (All Saints Division); Leonard Silverman, the town's leading solicitor; Arnold Beaton, the architect . . .

Now, in early October, many of the Parklands homes were shut up, windows closed, blinds drawn to shield expensive carpets from the sun, furniture dust-sheeted. Their owners were on holiday, motoring in Scotland, or perhaps pleasure cruising in the Mediterranean, though not many had ventured abroad this year. It seemed more prudent to stay in England until the Munich crisis "blew over."

Seven, Parklands, was the Stanford home. This afternoon the doors of the double garage were open wide, and a gleaming, dark-green Sunbeam Talbot with red-and-white L plates fixed to its bumpers was emerging cautiously, like a snail from its shell.

Pauline Stanford reversed slowly down in the driveway, with its border of geraniums, lobelia, and snow-in-summer. She knew perfectly well she should have a qualified driver beside her in the car—but her test was booked for tomorrow, she simply had to practice her corner-reversing and three-point turn, and there was no one available to come out with her. Her mother was at an afternoon bridge party, and those of her friends who could drive all seemed to be away on holiday. She had made Flora, her younger sister, promise not to tell anyone she had taken the car out on her own.

The Sunbeam Talbot smelled of new leather. It was brand-new, an eighteenth-birthday gift from her father. The shining polish and chrome hadn't seen so much as a spot of rain yet. Pauline had been taking driving lessons since the summer term ended at the High School. Her very last term! She was glad to have left, to have cast aside the navy-blue uniform and with it the stigma of "schoolgirl." She'd bought her first lipstick the other day from the cosmetics counter at Burridge's. She had wanted to leave school when she was sixteen, but her parents had decided she must stay another three terms. The headmistress had suggested Pauline might go on to the University; she had an aptitude for languages. But though Pauline enjoyed French and German with Miss Sinclair, who was young and different from most of the other mistresses, she didn't want to spend three years at college. Why, she'd be twenty-one by the time she finished studying. So old! And what use would a college degree be to her? She didn't need to earn her own living. . . . Pauline had enjoyed life this summer, doing the round of Renchester's social engagements. There was the tennis-club dance to look forward to next week, and then Tony Welsh's twenty-first party at the end of the month. . . .

Peering into the driving-mirror, she swerved into the road with a spurt of gravel. She was determined to pass her test tomorrow, partly because everyone said she'd never pull it off after only one course of lessons. She decided to practice reversing around the corner where the pillar-box stood—still with the monogram "ER" which for Edward VIII's brief reign had replaced the old "GR." Some day, perhaps, they would get around to changing it back to "GR" again. Pauline remembered clearly the discussions her parents had held about King Edward's abdication and his marriage to Mrs. Simpson. She wondered what it felt like to be Princess Elizabeth, to find yourself living in Buckingham Palace with your father unexpectedly crowned King of England, and to know that one day you would be Queen.

She drew up beside the pillar-box. The house on this corner belonged to the Mawtons. It had white-painted, farmhouse-style railings surrounding an impeccable lawn. "Green velvet" was the metaphor that sprang to the mind of every passer-by. Her first reverse was good, a hairbreadth from the curb all the way round. The second attempt wasn't so good—the tire of her nearside front wheel scraped the pavement. The third wasn't bad, a bit out into the center of the road. . . . She tried twice more, and managed to repeat her first performance.

Now for the three-point turn. The road just here was rather narrow; she thought she would practice that farther along. Handling the controls with too much confidence, she backed the car into the Mawtons' driveway, to head it in the right direction.

Then it happened. The way such things do happen—suddenly, inexplicably. There was the impact of collision, and a scrunching, tearing sound of wood. Pauline slammed down the footbrake, pulled on the handbrake, switched off the engine, and scrambled out to investigate. Heavens! She didn't know which was worse: the damage to her shiny new car—a long, crinkly dent in the offside mudguard, or the uprooted white gatepost that lay across the green velvet lawn.

She was still contemplating the disaster when the Mawtons' front door banged and she heard footsteps approaching. She grimaced. Old Henry Mawton had a reputation for being outspoken.

But it wasn't old Henry Mawton who appeared. It was his son. Pauline knew him by sight. She had heard he worked in the office at his father's factory. "Making money out of bottling colored water and putting a fizz in it," as her father had once remarked. Now, as he came up to the car, she saw again that he was tall and dark and had a pleasant, easygoing look about him.

"Well! That was quite a performance," he greeted her.

Pauline flushed, and tucked back a strand of her fair hair with a nervous gesture. "I'm sorry," she said briefly, then added unnecessarily: "it was an accident."

"I don't imagine you do that sort of thing on purpose."

"I'll—I'll pay for the gatepost, of course. I'm Pauline Stanford, by the way." She took it for granted that he would recognize the name: Stanford & Earle were the best known firm of estate agents in Renchester. Her father handled every important local property deal.

"I'm Clive Mawton—I say, it's tough about your car. New, isn't she?"

Hands in trouser pockets, Clive walked slowly round the Sunbeam Talbot.

Pauline felt ridiculous tears prickling her eyelids. Her beautiful new car! She nodded, and blew her nose. Then she was able to speak again.

"It's an absolutely maddening thing to have happened. I'm taking my test tomorrow." She frowned. "D'you think the examiner will give me a black mark for the dent?"

Clive shrugged. "There's no knowing how driving examiners' minds work. You'll have to ooze charm to offset the damage." He looked at Pauline coolly. "I'm sure he'll succumb. They prefer blondes."

"Oh." Pauline still felt at a loss when young men made remarks like that. They did, quite often, and Tony Welsh had kissed her when he saw her home after the last hunt ball. She was glad she'd used her new lipstick that afternoon, and felt vaguely sorry that the encounter with Clive Mawton couldn't be prolonged.

"Well"—she slid back into the driving-seat—"I'll expect the bill for the gatepost."

"Hey, just a minute——"

In the act of pulling the self-starter, Pauline looked up in surprise as Clive laid a hand on the steering wheel.

"Forgive me for pointing it out," he said with a grin, "but you're still in reverse gear."

Flustered already, Pauline felt this was the last straw. "Blast!" she muttered fiercely.

Clive looked at her consideringly. "Were you on your way to any definite destination?" he asked, tactfully ignoring the fact that she was an unaccompanied learner.

"I was just going to practice turning," Pauline replied, getting into first gear with a mild crash.

"Look—would you like me to come for a drive with you? I mean, this sort of contretemps"—he waved one hand towards the fallen gatepost—"is like falling off a horse. The best thing is to mount again as soon as possible."

"Haven't you anything else to do?" Pauline felt this sounded ungracious. Actually she was delighted by his offer. Perhaps they could go over the test route, which was up by the new housing estates.

"Actually, I have got a job on hand—I've to meet someone at the station, a chap from Germany who's coming to study our factory methods. I was just about to set off when I—er—heard you arrive."

He jerked his head in the direction of the house. Pauline noticed a sleek-looking Lagonda parked by the front door.

"If you wouldn't mind stopping by the station just to pick him up and deposit him at his digs, we could go over the test route afterwards," Clive went on.

"Of course. That would be marvelous. Um—*you'd* better drive to the station."

I certainly had, Clive thought to himself as he took the wheel while Pauline slid into the other front seat.

"Father will get a shock when he comes home and sees

the wreckage!" he said with a smile as they turned into St. Oswald's Terrace and headed downtown. "However, his bark is worse than his bite. He'll get over it." He looked at his watch. "Ten to four. The three-twenty from Crewe gets in at five past. We'll do it easily."

Pauline relaxed, enjoying being driven so competently. They passed the Eldorado cinema in the High Street. Coming next week . . . *Sixty Glorious Years*. She must see that. Everyone said Anna Neagle was perfect as Queen Victoria. They drove into the station yard as the Town Hall clock stuck four. Clive left Pauline in the car and went over to the ticket barrier. Presently she saw him returning with a slight, fair boy who was carrying a suitcase in one hand and a briefcase in the other.

"Herr Hoffman—Miss Stanford." Clive made the introductions, and the German acknowledged Pauline's smile with a stiff little bow.

They set off for the boardinghouse where Erich Hoffman was to stay, and as they drove out of the station yard, Pauline recognized a familiar figure in a blue coat and skirt, walking alongside an elderly man.

"There's old Doc Sinclair," Clive remarked. "That's his daughter with him, isn't it?"

Vernon Sinclair had been the Mawtons' family doctor for years.

"Miss Sinclair? Mmm. She teaches at school . . . the High School, I mean." She must get out of the habit of referring to school as though she were still a pupil there, Pauline told herself.

"Really?" Clive glanced quickly sideways at Suzanne's distant figure. "She looks too pretty for a schoolmarm."

In answer to Clive's polite, formal questions about his

journey, Erich Hoffman made polite, formal answers. Yes, it had been a good crossing. No, the train journey had been without difficulty. Yes, he felt ready for something to eat. He was also looking forward with much eagerness to studying the new methods employed in the Mawton factory. He wondered whether Clive would be interested to see a pamphlet he had been reading on the train about the latest developments in fruit-juice extractors. . . .

"Not just at this moment, old man," Clive said, drawing up outside the boardinghouse, where a discreet notice in one corner of a lace-curtained window advertised "Vacancies." "Some other time, eh?"

They left Erich in the care of a kindly landlady with a Renchester accent so broad that the German could hardly understand one word she spoke.

"These Germans—so earnest about everything," Clive commented as he handed over the wheel to Pauline, and she drove off in the direction of the new estates.

They spent an hour and a half going over the test route, reversing, turning, practicing the emergency stop, and the hill start. Privately, Clive had doubts about whether Pauline would pass the test tomorrow, but he managed to sound encouraging about her chances when she asked him. He enjoyed the drive: she was an attractive girl; he thought he would like to know her better. When they returned to Parklands, he made a date with her for the following week. They were to see *Sixty Glorious Years* together.

Pauline returned home feeling elated. She hadn't imagined she would find a new boy friend that afternoon! She decided to break the news to her father about the dent in the car after dinner that evening. Wasn't there some old saying about people taking bad news better after they'd eaten? "A hungry man is an angry man"—perhaps that was what she was thinking of.

In the hall she met Flora.

"Who was that in the car with you?" Flora asked.

"Clive Mawton," Pauline replied self-consciously. "I knocked down his father's fence and smashed up my car."

"What!" Flora, who had a literal mind, looked horrified.

Pauline threw her cashmere cardigan onto a chair. "Not really. That was a slight exaggeration. You're not to say anything to Mummy or Daddy, mind. I'm going to tell them about it after we've eaten."

And leaving Flora to speculate on how anyone could possibly be so cheerful after such disaster, Pauline ran upstairs to change.

Shorthand Typist

⌒

Marion Gray hurried back to her typist's desk at Stanford & Earle, Estate Agents, at the end of her lunch hour. She almost ran along the High Street, past the Gas Showrooms, Burton the Fifty Shilling Tailor, Prendergast's, the piano and sheet music shop, and Marks and Spencer (Nothing Over Five Shillings). In one hand she clutched a paper bag that held her sister's birthday present. Eva wanted a workbox, and Marion had found just the thing: a square basket lined with padded cotton and equipped with scissors, reels of cotton, a darning egg, and packets of pins and needles. Quite good value for five shillings, she thought. The word "Foreign" was stamped on the base of the basket. Made in Japan, most likely. Marion had a vague picture of sweated labor in a kimono. Japan and China were countries so far away that they seemed almost lands of the imagination. Of course, Marion knew that war had been raging in China for two years now, ever since the Japanese invaded

35

Manchuria in 1936. Even so, she found it difficult to replace the romantic pictures of almond blossoms, rickshaws, and paper houses conjured up in her mind by the word Japan with scenes of modern warfare: bombs, shells, and devastated rice fields.

She paused to look in the office window before going inside. The showcard advertising Briardale House occupied a prominent position. A glossy photograph, taken from a flattering angle, was stuck onto an oblong of pasteboard. Underneath was the advertisement she had typed out that morning:

Just on the market
BRIARDALE HOUSE
In unspoiled countryside within easy reach of Renchester,
a gentleman's residence in secluded grounds
This desirable freehold property
FOR SALE
with immediate possession
Sole Agents: Stanford & Earle

Desirable property! Marion thought grimly. They'd be lucky to get that barracks of a place off their hands in a hurry. Mr. Stanford himself had gone to inspect the house, and Marion had accompanied him to take notes. "Unspoiled countryside": that meant cesspool drainage, an unreliable electric generator in the grounds, and a three-mile trek to the nearest shop. The "secluded grounds" had long since run to seed. All this, together with ten bedrooms, four reception rooms, staff accommodation and no central heating, did not, in Marion's opinion, make a desirable property. But still—the place

had a curious charm. It was easy to tell that once it had
been a lovely house, in the days when there were plenty
of gardeners to tend the grounds and indoor servants to
scrub and polish, fetch and carry. It had been obvious
that Lady Cortley, the present owner, was sad to let the
place go. But death duties and rising income tax had
deprived her of the means to keep Briardale House in
proper style. There was nothing for it but to sell—if she
could. Mr. Stanford had made it quite plain that the
house might remain on the market for some time.

Marion had been impressed by Lady Cortley, a gentle
yet lively minded woman in her fifties. She was a widow,
and only three months ago her son, Gavin, had been
killed in Spain.

Gavin Cortley had joined the International Brigade,
formed by volunteers from different countries to fight
with the Spanish Republicans in their Civil War against
the Fascist Party, led by General Franco. He was machine-gunned from a Nazi plane during a Republican
counterattack across the river Ebro. Nazi Germany and
Fascist Italy had supported General Franco; Communist
Russia had sent aid to the Republicans.

Marion had sensed that Lady Cortley was not a woman
to resign herself to a meek role of bereaved wife and
mother. A recent photograph in the *Renchester Echo*
had shown her in the Town Hall, receiving parcels of
clothing for refugees. She was on the committee of the
Central Refugee Relief Organization, formed to help
refugees from Hitler's persecution of Jews and anti-Nazis
in Germany, Austria, and the Sudetenland. She had conducted their tour of Briardale House in a practical,
efficient manner, but every now and then she had con-

jured up, in reminiscent phrases, the days of prosperity
when she had come there as a bride at the turn of the
century.

"The Briardale roses were famous. We used to give a
garden party each year when they were at their best,"
she said, as they stood in the midst of a sunken garden
where grass grew rankly and flower beds and paths were
obliterated by long neglect.

Again: "We always kept a huge log fire burning here
in the winter"—this as she threw open the door of the
empty library, which even on that summer day felt cold
and cheerless.

But to Marion, her remarks had seemed to bring back
something of the color and movement of Edwardian
garden parties held in honor of the white and yellow
roses, and to fan to life firelight glowing on shelves filled
with leather-bound books.

Marion's boss, John Stanford, would have been surprised to know her thoughts. As far as he was concerned,
Marion scarcely had a personality; with her shorthand
notebook and typewriter, she formed a sort of combined
office unit. He knew she lived with her family somewhere
downtown; that the headmaster of the elementary school
she had attended until she was fourteen, and the principal of Pitman's College, where she received her secretarial training, had given her good references. He knew,
too, that during the eighteen months she had worked in
the office she had proved herself a conscientious employee.
He supposed she would stay with the firm a few years,
then leave to get married, whereupon he would engage
another shorthand typist in her place. If someone had
said to him, "Marion Gray is the same age as your

daughter Pauline," he would have been surprised. It simply did not occur to him to place his typist and his daughter in a related thought sequence.

His outline of knowledge about Marion was accurate so far as it went. The Grays did live downtown, in Povey Street, which, though respectable, had seen better days. Marion's father, Thomas Gray, was employed in a printing works. He was one of those little men who seem to try to make up for their lack of stature by a hectoring manner. He was a Socialist, and frequently aired his political opinions. Yet at the same time he had a curious streak of snobbery. His Socialist convictions had grown out of a sense of grievance that his lot was humble, rather than a sincere belief in the equality of mankind. While professing to despise the aristocratic tradition, he cherished an ill-founded legend handed down from his paternal grandfather, that he was descended from noble blood.

Marion's mother was an easygoing woman who took her husband's bullying in good part. On rare occasions she was able to tease him into a frame of mind where he could laugh at himself; and then, briefly, she glimpsed again the outspoken printer's apprentice she had first met in her girlhood at gatherings of the local reading circle, when he had impressed her with long quotations from the writings of H. G. Wells.

Eva Gray, Marion's sister, was twenty. She worked for Madame Rita, a hairdresser in the High Street. Her chief interests lay in Ken Martin, a Povey Street boy with whom she was "going steady," and the cinema, particularly the films of Robert Taylor and Gary Cooper. Every Saturday night, Ken called for Eva in his best blue

suit, with his hair slicked down until it looked like black
patent leather. Then they set off on his motorbike for
the Odeon, or the Eldorado, or the Granada, and sat in
the warm darkness holding hands and smoking Wood-
bines.

John Stanford's easy supposition that Marion would
soon settle down into conventional domesticity was not
shared by Marion herself. She was ambitious. Not for
her, marriage with someone like Ken Martin, a bungalow
furnished on the hire purchase, a secondhand car for
weekend outings, and two or three squalling kids. Life
must hold more than that for Marion Gray. She felt she
deserved, by virtue of her intelligence, to belong uptown.
Somehow she was determined to break loose from her
downtown background. She had wanted to go on to
secondary school, but in Povey Street it was taken for
granted that you earned your own living by the time you
were sixteen at least—especially if you were a girl. She'd
been considered bright at school, and could have won a
scholarship to the High School. She knew this, and it
rankled. She had found her secretarial training boring,
but knew she needed shorthand, typing, and bookkeep-
ing if she was ever to "get anywhere." She had answered
an advertisement in the *Echo* for the job with Stanford
& Earle, and although her own work in the office was
purely routine, she found the business of an estate agency
interesting.

Marion did not have a boy friend. The youths of her
neighborhood, sensing her indifference to them, thought
twice about dating her. And there seemed no opportunity
to meet other young men socially.

Now she opened the heavy glass door that shut out

the traffic of the High Street, and went through to the little cubicle, partitioned off from the main office, which she shared with Geoff Chanter, Mr. Stanford's junior clerk. Geoff was eating sandwiches at his desk, and reading a textbook of land law. He was studying for the exams of the Chartered Auctioneers' and Estate Agents' Institute, going to evening classes at the technical college.

"Hallo," he greeted Marion. "On the dot as usual. Punctual as a blooming clock, you are."

Marion took off her hat (Mr. Stanford liked his female staff to wear hats) and put her parcel in a drawer of her desk. Then she sat down at her typewriter. There were half a dozen letters in her notebook still to be typed, the residue of the morning's dictation sessions with her boss.

"It's a wonder you don't get sick of bloater paste," she remarked, wrinkling her nose and tucking a sheet of headed paper into the machine.

"My mum has a one-track mind," Geoff replied cheerfully. "S'matter of fact, she bought a half gross of bloater paste last month—special cut-price offer at the grocer's."

Marion smiled. She had an attractive smile that appeared too seldom.

"That's better," Geoff said. "I like it when you smile. Sometimes you sit tapping away at that typewriter with such a poker face, it worries me. Life ain't all that serious!"

Geoff was quite fond of young Marion. (He was four or five years older than she was.) Marion, for her part, sometimes found his flippant manner irritating, but on the whole he was an easy person with whom to share a small office.

"Anything happen while I was out?" she asked, starting on her first letter. (*Dear Sir, In reply to your communication of the 15th inst. regarding the auction sale to be conducted at 46 Colnbrook Avenue . . .*)

"Nothing world-shattering . . . the boss's daughter blew in, full of joy about her driving test. She passed it this morning, apparently."

"Oh?" Marion knew Pauline Stanford well enough by sight. She felt a mixture of envy and contempt for the carefree life she led up at Parklands.

"Nice little car she's got," Geoff went on. "She parked it just outside. It had a great bash in one mudguard, though. Shame—brand-new it looked otherwise. She had a smooth-looking chap with her. Lounge-lizard type."

Marion shrugged. "I can't understand how girls like Pauline Stanford fill up their time. I mean, what does she do all day? Besides passing her driving test, of course. I'd want to get myself a job, if I was her."

Geoff looked up at the sharp tone that had crept into Marion's voice. "Funny, the way people are always saying 'if I were you' when what they really mean is 'if you were me,'" he remarked.

Marion sensed the rebuke in this, and concentrated on the letter she was typing. (*. . . shall be pleased to meet you at a date mutually convenient to us both. Yours truly . . .*) Oh, heck, she'd mis-typed *mutually*. Why should the casual mention of Pauline Stanford's "nice little car" and her "smooth-looking chap" make her feel so sore? Crossly, she reached for her eraser, then had second thoughts, tore the sheet of paper from her machine, and began the letter again. Mr. Stanford had an eagle eye for erasures. Might as well do it again now as have it sent back for retyping later on. . . .

Outside, in the High Street, the tide of Renchester life flowed on, reaching out to every quarter of the town.

A few doors along from Stanford & Earle's offices, Suzanne Sinclair was giving her weekly grocery order to an assistant in Clark's main store—the one who had once had an accident with the bacon slicer and had been stitched up by her father. Ever since that event, he had liked to see to Miss Sinclair's order himself.

Across the suspension bridge, down by the docks, Erich Hoffman, visitor from Germany, wandered purposefully with his camera, taking shots according to his instructions. There seemed to him to be little shipbuilding of any significance in progress here, however; nothing to compare with the pocket battleships and U-boats being built with such efficiency for the *Führer's* arms program. He thought of the mighty *Tirpitz,* pride of the German navy.

Up at Parklands, Mrs. Stanford made the arrangements for her Saturday afternoon bridge party, setting out cards and markers. Pauline helped her rather absent-mindedly, thinking about Clive Mawton. She had passed him in the High Street that morning, and he had waved to her and then come with her to tell her father the good news about the driving test.

Over on one of the new housing estates, in a semi-detached house faced with mock-Tudor beams—number 8, Laburnum Close—Mary, the girl who had been too diffident to eat her cheese-and-pickle sandwiches in the train, was in the middle of her second day as general maidservant. She stood in the kitchen gazing admiringly at the refrigerator purring so mysteriously in one corner. Fancy working in a house with a refrigerator! Imagine not having to stand the butter and milk in earthenware jars of cold water to keep them from going off! The mistress had told her to defrost the strange machine and clean it out. She opened the door nervously. . . .

In the offices of the *Renchester Echo,* sub-editors sorted out the week's news, scandal, and gossip, gathered in from every district: the report of the latest Town Council meeting; the inquiry into the bypass dispute; the wedding photographs and paragraphs (indistinguishable, to a stranger's eye, from those of last week and the week before); the small ads, the announcements of births and deaths, the In Memoriam messages . . . The editor had prepared a leader which began with some reflections on the Munich Pact, and ended with an exhortation to the Renchester Councillors to hasten the completion of the town's slum-resettlement scheme.

Renchester—Britain—the world itself—had traveled a week closer to the horizon of war.

Invitation

The sale of Briardale House was completed much sooner than anyone expected. The buyer was Henry Mawton. It so happened that his grandfather, the founder of the mineral water factory, had been born in a cottage on the grounds of Briardale House—son of Samuel Mawton, head gardener to Sir Gavin Cortley, the fourth baronet. Samuel Mawton had been an excellent gardener. It was he who founded the famous rose beds, in the year his son was born, a decade after Waterloo.

Perhaps the green-fingered shade of Samuel Mawton, disturbed by the neglected state of the once carefully tended grounds, prompted his great-grandson to buy the house.

It was Clive who had brought home the news that Briardale House was up for sale. He knew the story of his gardening ancestor, and he tossed off the information as an incidental topic of conversation over dinner. ("By the way, there's an advertisement in Stanford & Earle's window for Briardale House.") His father, chewing on

45

roast beef, digested the news along with his meat. Then
—"How would you like to be mistress of Briardale House,
love?" he had asked his wife later in the evening.

"You're not serious, Harry," Lily Mawton had answered, dipping her fingers into a box of chocolate
creams.

She was a good-natured woman whose origins were
similar to those of her husband. Her father had made a
fortune out of jam. Parklands society recognized her
good nature, and she was popular in spite of the fact
that she was such an appalling bridge player. Although
she wore the most expensive clothes from Burridge's
model department, she never looked well dressed—a fact
closely connected with her addiction to chocolates. She
was in her element in household matters; at preserving
time her fruit-bottling and jam-making activities almost
reached the scale of her father's commercial beginnings.

"You don't really mean it, Harry," she had repeated.

But Henry Mawton was serious; he did mean it. And
so Briardale House was sold a month after it came into
the market, to the mutual satisfaction of Lady Julia
Cortley, Messrs. Stanford & Earle, and Henry Mawton
himself.

In eight months, the house had undergone a transformation as complete as Cinderella's in the pantomime.
The outside was repainted, brickwork repointed, the
terrace repaved, and the roof repaired. The inside was
redecorated and filled with new curtains, carpets, and
furniture. A cocktail bar was installed at one end of the
library; the former servants' hall had been turned into
a billiard room. Central heating was put in, and the
kitchen was equipped with the latest gadgets. The grounds

were newly landscaped, the lawns returfed, herbaceous borders restocked, and the rose beds restored to something approaching their former glory. Indoors, everything gleamed and shone and smelled of new paint and polish. Outside, all was pruned and weeded and in good order. Henry and Lily Mawton felt secure within their castle.

In June, 1939, they sent out invitations to a housewarming to be held later in the month. Nearly all those wealthy and influential members of Renchester society were invited, and most of them accepted. As the evening of the party drew near, they looked forward with lively curiosity to seeing Mawton's Folly, as many had rechristened Briardale House. For in that summer of glorious weather and perilous politics, it seemed a most ill-chosen time to set oneself up as lord of a manor. Worldly Rencastrians were astonished that a man of Henry Mawton's business acumen could be so foolhardy. But Henry Mawton himself did not share the general pessimism over the political situation. The metamorphosis of Briardale House was a practical demonstration of his conviction that there would not be a European war.

It must have been the prevailing mood of uncertainty which accounted for the fact that the Mawtons' Parklands house stood empty, still seeking a buyer, several months after the family had moved into their new home. *4 Parklands—An architect-designed modern house in a most favored residential district* stayed on the For Sale list with Stanford & Earle. Now it was the turn of that gabled villa to suffer decay. The rooms grew cold and damp. Chickweed sprouted in the graveled driveway. The green velvet lawn was disfigured by clumps of clover and celandine.

Lack of confidence in what tomorrow would bring was the reason put forward by John Stanford for the non-sale of the house, in an interview with Henry Mawton one morning.

"As you know yourself, Mawton, normally these Parklands properties are snapped up as soon as they become available," he told his client. "But at the present time prospective buyers are holding back. I suppose the possibility of having a bomb dropped through a newly acquired roof isn't exactly encouraging. . . ."

In one corner of the office, Marion was filing letters, a model of silent efficiency. She was glad, for Lady Cortley's sake, that the sale of Briardale House had gone off so smoothly. Mr. Mawton hadn't haggled over the price; he was a man who knew what he wanted, and was willing —and able—to pay for it. Marion would have liked to see what the Mawtons had made of the place. It must look very different from the way it did when Lady Cortley had shown them round last year. She slipped a file of inventories into its proper place, keeping an ear open to the conversation between the two men.

Henry Mawton, with a benevolent expression on his face, was sitting back in his chair. He didn't seem very worried by the non-sale of the Parklands house.

"I can afford to wait; people will come to their senses sooner or later," he told John Stanford. "There isn't going to be a war, you know."

Marion could tell that Mr. Stanford found it hard to swallow this easy assurance.

"It's a good house and I want a fair price for it," Henry Mawton continued. "I won't sell to anyone who thinks he can get it on the cheap because of this war scare."

"Well, well, we must wait and see. I can only assure you that we'll do our best for you." Mr. Stanford concluded the interview on this indefinite note, and his client got up from his chair.

"By the way—my wife and I and Pauline, of course— are looking forward to your housewarming. It's to be quite an occasion by all accounts."

"Oh, aye. Lily—my wife—is full of it. Daft carry-on in a sense: you spend a mint of money on new carpets, then invite a lot of folks to come and spill drink and drop cigar ash all over 'em. That reminds me—I must ask my secretary what she's done about booking the band for the dancing. The young folks expect that, you know! I like a waltz myself, come to that." Then he looked at John Stanford and said meaningly: "I've no doubt our Clive will be asking your Pauline for a good few dances."

John Stanford was embarrassed by this outspoken reference to the friendship between Clive Mawton and his daughter. He wasn't sure that he liked the notion underlying Henry Mawton's words—the notion of an alliance between the two young people. Plenty of money there, of course—but then money wasn't everything.

"No doubt," he replied formally, remembering too that Miss Gray was in the office. Small-town gossip could marry couples off before they'd even met. "Er—I shall look forward to seeing your improvements to Briardale House. I'm sure it must be very much changed from the time Miss Gray and I went down to look over it last year." He smiled at Marion kindly.

She was surprised to be taken notice of: it was rather as though someone had suddenly pushed forward a pet dog to be patted on the head. She half smiled nervously.

Henry Mawton turned to her. "Oh, so you saw the place as it was before we moved in, Miss—er, Miss Gray, did you?" And then he came out with a characteristic gesture, which, though well-meant, was ill-considered. "In that case," he said, "you must come along to our housewarming. There'll be plenty of other young people there; it won't all be old fogeys like myself and Mr. Stanford here!"

Marion gasped. "Oh—that's—that's very kind of you, I'm sure, Mr. Mawton. I—I——"

"That's settled, then. We'll look forward to seeing you." And bidding Mr. Stanford good-by, Henry Mawton left the office.

"Well, Miss Gray, that was an unexpected invitation," her employer remarked, handing her the file for 4, Parklands.

"Yes, Mr. Stanford. Er—do you think he really meant it? I mean, will he really expect to see me there? I don't even know what date it is."

John Stanford raised his eyebrows. This was tiresome. "I'm sure Mr. Mawton is not the sort of person to issue an invitation he didn't mean. No doubt you will receive a formal invitation card tomorrow. He has a reputation for being a man of his word, you know."

Marion noticed that Mr. Stanford didn't urge her to go to the party. No doubt he felt she would be out of place there, out of her element—her downtown element. The "other young people," Clive Mawton's friends, would not be her sort of young people. They would be Pauline

Stanford's sort. Well, it would be easy enough to make up an excuse and say she couldn't go, after all. . . .

Mr. Stanford obviously considered the discussion closed. He reached for the telephone and asked the operator to get him a number.

Marion returned to her filing; and, quite suddenly, she decided that she would accept Mr. Mawton's invitation. She would go to the party at Briardale House. Why shouldn't she? She might have been a High School girl, just like Pauline Stanford. . . . Besides, she did want to see what changes had been made to the house and in the grounds. She'd heard that the rose garden was in bloom again. That would be a heavenly place on a June evening, a romantic place. . . .

A Family Called Jelinck

Committee meetings of the Central Refugee Relief Organization were held in London. Julia Cortley was a member of a residential club for gentlewomen close by the offices of the C.R.R.O., where she stayed overnight whenever she traveled from Renchester for the meetings.

Today, she was lunching in the club dining room with an old friend who was also on the committee. Mildred Lyall, an affluent spinster, lived in London and devoted her money and her energy to deserving causes.

"I'm glad we've been able to do something for that family called Jelinck," Julia Cortley was saying. "The work we've arranged for the father will at least enable him to keep some self-respect. And it is connected with music."

"Somewhat tenuously," Mildred murmured, sipping sherry. "Piano tuning in Renchester is quite a comedown after leading the Prague Conservatoire Orchestra—to put it mildly." She was privately amused by the way in which

Julia used the plural personal pronoun in such a regal manner—or did she do so from a sense of modesty? It had been she alone who had dealt with the case of the Jelinck family.

"It's a tragedy his bowing arm is so affected," Mildred went on.

"A form of nervous paralysis, they say. He had to give up the violin three months ago. He'd been playing in some restaurant orchestra, background music for food and gossip."

Mildred sighed. "Tragic: terrible: disastrous. All the adjectives seem inadequate to describe the way these people have had their whole lives wrecked. Every aspect —families broken up, homes gone, careers finished, dispossessed of their nationality. Yet it's becoming such a commonplace occurrence that there's a danger, it seems to me, of taking the refugee's plight almost for granted. We're approaching the stage where we accept him as a natural phenomenon of Europe, as typical as *apfelstrudel* or *wurst*."

Julia Cortley picked up her soup spoon. "There have always been refugees—Jews, Huguenots, White Russians . . . but never on such a wholesale scale. I must admit I sometimes find the number of cases on our lists daunting. There seems no end to it. To revert to the Jelinck family—the house the council has offered them is on one of those new estates on the outskirts of Renchester."

Mildred crumbled a bread roll. "How did you find the job for Josef Jelinck?"

"When I moved from Briardale I sold the Steinway through old Prendergast—he's our leading music dealer. He happened to mention that his regular piano tuner and

repairer was retiring. I thought of Jelinck at once, and
Prendergast was eager to help. I only hope it all works
out all right. Needless to say, the voting at the council
meeting wasn't unanimously in favor of offering the
house to a refugee family. You can see why there would
be objections—Renchester has plenty of slums awaiting
clearance, after all."

She consulted the choice of entrees on the menu. "Are
you having the lamb or the gammon?" she asked Mildred.

"The lamb, I think."

Julia Cortley said thoughtfully: "I don't quite know
what my attitude to the British would be if I were a
Czech refugee. I might, I suppose, feel considerable
bitterness, having watched Mr. Chamberlain fly to
Munich and dispose of my country in order to preserve
peace for other people."

The lamb arrived. Mildred helped herself to red-currant
jelly. "Of course," she said, "at the time of Munich we
genuinely thought we were giving away the smaller
portion—the Sudetenland—in order to save the greater.
We couldn't foresee that six months later Hitler would
seize the rest of Czechoslovakia."

"If I were a Czech, I think I might find it difficult to
understand such lack of foresight." Julia Cortley's
thoughts reverted to the Jelincks. "Anna Jelinck, the
daughter, is eleven. A place has been arranged for her
at the High School. An anonymous donor provided
quite a large sum for her education. I have reason to
believe it may have been a Renchester solicitor called
Leonard Silverman—a Jew. He's very interested in our
organization."

"I wonder how she will fit in with Renchester school-girls?"

"Luckily the whole family speaks English fairly well. There was a son, you know—Tomas. He was a student at the University in Prague. He . . . disappeared . . . when the Germans occupied Prague. Hundreds of students were shot or taken to concentration camps."

It occurred to Mildred that Julia and the mother of Tomas Jelinck had experienced a similar tragedy: the loss of an only son. She knew Julia was proud that Gavin had died fighting for his belief in freedom, his hatred of tyranny.

When in January that year, Generalissimo Franco had captured Barcelona, the Catalan army had surrendered—and the following month, Britain formally recognized Franco's regime—Julia Cortley's pride had saved her from feeling that Gavin's death had been in vain. Now that a much closer war seemed imminent, she realized that Gavin's belief in freedom, strong enough to compel him to take up arms, would be demonstrated by millions of other men and women. In a sense, Gavin's death was in anticipation of all those others to come.

Tomas Jelinck's fate was not known for sure. The Jelinck family—father, mother, and daughter—had fled to London from Prague in March, when Hitler extended his "protection" beyond the Sudetenland and the boundaries fixed in the Munich Agreement, to the rest of Czechoslovakia. Josef Jelinck had played sub-principal violin in the Conservatoire Orchestra. Tomas had been studying philosophy at the Charles University; Anna Jelinck was at school in Prague. They had arrived in

England destitute, lucky to have escaped with their lives.
Immediately after the Nazi invasion of the rest of
Czechoslovakia, the Gestapo had launched its customary
pogroms against the Jewish and anti-Nazi sections of
the population. There had been mass shootings and de-
portations. Now, after several months of hand-to-mouth
existence, the Jelincks hoped they might be able to build
up a new life for themselves, however incongruous a setting the provincial town of Renchester might seem for
them.

Over coffee after lunch, the conversation between the
two women turned to Julia Cortley's new house. Bay
Tree Cottage was in a village not far from Briardale
House.

"And how is the Mineral Water magnate getting on
at Briardale?" Mildred asked.

"Splendidly, by all accounts. He's installed a cocktail
bar in the library—how Hugo would have shuddered!—a
billiard room in the servants' hall (they'd have liked
that), and the rose gardens are in order again. For that,
I forgive him the cocktail bar. Actually, they're about to
throw a huge housewarming. I was terrified they would
invite me. Luckily they've been tactful enough not to do
so." She poured out more coffee. "Really, I'm happy to
think of them there. I'm only sorry they may very soon
find themselves having to cope with all sorts of un-
imagined difficulties. Running Briardale in wartime
wouldn't be an easy task. As it is, their under-gardener
has already been called up."

In April, following the Nazi annexation of the rest of
Czechoslovakia, and Italy's invasion of Albania on Good
Friday that year, the Government had announced that

conscription was to be introduced. A few weeks later, military training became compulsory for young men not in "reserved occupations"—that is, occupations considered essential by the Government for the smooth working of the community. It seemed that at last (too late, the pessimists declared) Britain was aroused to the full danger of Nazi ambition. To deter Hitler from further aggression, the Government had guaranteed Poland, Greece, and Rumania, and had signed a friendship pact with Turkey. If any of these countries were attacked, Britain was committed to go to their support and to declare war on Germany.

"The way the country has accepted conscription is a very different story from 1916," Mildred went on. There was an undertone of sadness in her voice. In 1916 she had been engaged to be married to Eddie Carlisle. Eddie had enlisted in 1914; he was killed a few weeks after they had announced their engagement. Mildred remembered the bitterness she had felt, shared by other soldiers' relatives, when men who had been wounded two or three times over returned to the front to fight on, while others stayed at home in their civilian occupations. That situation had finally been altered by the introduction of conscription in 1916, but even then, after two years of war, the necessity for conscription had not been accepted as it was today.

Julia Cortley guessed that Mildred was thinking of Eddie.

"The issues at stake today are so much clearer," she said gently. "The 1914 war was directed by our political leaders; the people were out of touch with international events. This time it seems as though it is the people who are taking the lead, urging on our politicians. The evil of Nazism is plain for all of us to see."

Mildred decided it was time they changed the subject. One had so many conversations about war these days: the possibility of war, the impossibility of war, the certainty of war. . . . Rumors of poison gas, germ warfare, high-explosive bombs. . . . All these were common topics. It was very depressing.

"We've just time to find a taxi and get to the theater in good time," she said firmly. "I always like to read the program properly before the curtain goes up."

Julia Cortley smiled and obediently abandoned her coffee cup. Outside, the sun was shining. They walked towards a nearby square where the plane trees were in their summer foliage. Here Mildred hailed a taxi, and they drove off to a matinee of *French Without Tears*, which everyone said was so witty and so charming: just the thing to make one forget about Hitler.

Housewarming

The syncopated moan of dance music floated from the open windows of the library at Briardale House. Benny Lewis and his boys, the fashionable local band, came to the end of a sentimental waltz, then changed smartly into the brisker rhythm of one of the latest hit tunes, "I Get Along Without You Very Well . . ."

Henry Mawton stood by the cocktail bar, watching the dancers glide over the polished floor. "Well, love," he said to his wife, "you know what they say—it takes three generations to make a gentleman. I'd like to see my great-grandfather's face tonight!"

Lily Mawton was looking disapprovingly at Cynthia Beaton's low-backed dress of silver lamé, as she quick-stepped her way around the room with Percy Harriman.

"A woman of her age, with a grown-up daughter, wearing a dress like that!" she remarked.

Lily herself was upholstered in midnight-blue lace. Cynthia Beaton, the wife of the architect, was different from the other wives of the Parklands circle. And this was Lily's true objection to her. Cynthia was a Londoner by birth—Arnold Beaton had met her there in his student days. She had a reputation for wearing dashing clothes, and holding "odd" opinions. Esmé, the Beatons' seventeen-year-old daughter, had not gone to the High School, like the other Parklands girls, but to a boarding school in the south.

"I still wish we'd asked Lady Cortley to the party," Henry Mawton declared, acknowledging a coy wave of the hand from Tobias Clark's wife, who was dancing with Leonard Silverman, the solicitor.

"No, Harry, it wouldn't have been right," Lily replied, with unusual vigor in her voice. But she could not have explained why she felt instinctively that to have invited the former chatelaine of Briardale House to the party would have been a mistake.

She looked across the crowded room and saw Marion Gray standing alone.

"I must find a partner for that young girl from John Stanford's office," she said, glancing round to see which young men were available. She caught Tony Welsh's eye. He would do. . . .

Pauline and Clive were strolling along the terrace, where tubs of sweet-scented geraniums had been placed at mathematically regular intervals. Clive was enjoying the party. Splendid the way his old man had branched out like this! Their new home was certainly making everyone take notice. The exclamations and secret calculations as to how much the transformation of Briardale

House had cost his father had scarcely died down yet, and the party was well under way now. It was fun being with Pauline, too, knowing she was the most attractive girl there, and that everyone thought of her as his girl friend. However, just at this moment, he wasn't too happy about the trend their conversation was taking. He hadn't known Pauline in this mood before. She seemed restless, and insisted on talking seriously, when all he wanted tonight was to dance, to flirt a little, to enjoy the party.

Now Pauline withdrew her arm from his to spread both hands wide in a gesture that emphasized what she was saying. "It doesn't seem enough, now, to go on leading the sort of life I've had since I left school. At first I enjoyed it, but now I'm sick of tennis-club dances, and morning coffee-parties, the gossip, and choosing new clothes at Burridge's. It's all so—empty. Perhaps I should have gone to college—that's what they wanted me to do at school."

"You—a bluestocking?" Clive exclaimed. He glanced down at her dance frock. "Blue tulle suits you better."

"Everything in Renchester is so conventional, so narrow," Pauline went on. "You meet the same little circle of people all the time. I feel as though I should like to escape."

Clive looked at her sideways, phrasing his next remark carefully. He didn't want to be taken up on it—not just yet, anyway.

"Perhaps you're the sort of girl who marries young," he said.

Pauline shook her head quickly, shying away from the

idea. "I don't think so! I don't want to settle down yet—I don't feel I've lived enough!"

"Well, what d'you propose to do about this state of affairs?" Clive took her hand firmly in his and directed their steps indoors. The band was playing "Lady, Be Good," and he wanted to dance.

"I thought I might take a secretarial course and then find some job in London. That's what Esmé Beaton's going to do. She and I were discussing it the other day. We even thought we might share a flat together . . ."

" 'Oh, sweet and lovely . . . ,' " Clive hummed softly in her ear as they drifted onto the dance floor. Then Pauline's words penetrated the tune and he repeated, startled: "London!"

They danced in silence for a moment.

"And Esmé Beaton!" Clive went on in astonishment. "She's not your type!"

Pauline sighed as her feet automatically performed the patterns of the quickstep. She caught sight of a girl called Sheila Collins, dancing rather well and looking glamorous. Sheila had belonged to Pauline's year at the High School—she'd been secretary of the League of Nations Club, Pauline remembered, and was now up at Oxford. *She* certainly didn't look bluestockingish!

Then Esmé swept past, performing sophisticated variations with one of her father's architectural assistants, a personable young man called Jim Hartley.

"Hallo, you two!" she called gaily as they met Clive and Pauline in the dance. "Jimmy's just been telling me he's a pacifist! None of this nonsense about fighting for King and Country, and all that!"

Clive looked shocked, and Pauline smiled inanely, not quite knowing how to take this.

"It's not a joke, you flippant creature!" Jim was heard to protest half seriously as he and Esmé floated away again.

How vivacious Esmé was! She would be a marvelous companion in London, Pauline thought. London . . . Clive had pronounced the word as though it were Timbuktu, and had spoken of Esmé as though she were a member of the International Set, or something! Pauline realized that Clive was part of her general dissatisfaction with life. He meant well, he was nice, good-looking, and it had been fun getting to know him, and rather exciting—at first. But now . . . well, she simply found him boring. *Boring*.

Marion was glad she had come. It was fascinating to see the house so changed, and a new experience for her to be among a throng of well-to-do Rencastrians. All the nobs were here! She'd tasted her first cocktail, too, a gin-and-lime, and there'd been an exhilarating moment when Tom Harris, the clarinet player in Benny Lewis's band, had recognized her. Tom lived in Povey Street. His face, when he'd spotted her! He'd nearly missed his cue, he was so surprised.

She thought her dress didn't compare too unfavorably with the other girls'. She'd bought it last week, recklessly laying out a third of her weekly wage at the Guinea Dress Shop. It was pink taffeta, the skirt overlaid with pink net. A pity the net had got a bit crushed from sitting on the pillion of Ken Martin's motorbike. . . .

It was her sister Eva who had suggested Ken should bring her to the party, and collect her again afterwards. He was to call for her a little after midnight.

Marion was not to know that Ken had only agreed to do this because he would do anything for his Evie. He didn't like Marion very much; he thought her a bit "stuck-up," not a patch on Evie.

Eva had lent Marion her *diamanté* necklace and ear-rings, too, and had done her hair, setting it in neat, corrugated waves in the best Madame Rita style. All in all, Marion felt very satisfied with the way she looked.

She'd seen Mr. and Mrs. Stanford, and her employer had greeted her and hoped she was enjoying herself. (After the encounter, Margaret Stanford had asked her husband, eyebrows raised, "What on earth is she doing here?"—her voice expressing her opinion of Marion's hectic pink frock, cheap jewelry, and downtown accent.)

It was this downtown accent which was to spoil the evening for Marion. It wouldn't have mattered so much if she'd been older: Tobias Clark, Percy Harriman and their wives—Henry and Lily Mawton themselves—spoke much the way Marion did. But not the younger set; they had what Marion thought of as BBC voices.

She was pleased when Mrs. Mawton introduced her to Tony Welsh. She knew him by sight; she'd seen him driving about in a red sports car, and there'd been a photograph of him in the *Echo,* she remembered, when he'd won the Tennis Club championship. He was a good dancer, she discovered; after "Lady, Be Good" there was another quickstep—"A Little Bit Independent." Tony crooned the words softly to himself.

Actually, Tony Welsh wasn't feeling too cheerful. He'd spent most of the evening gazing wistfully at Pauline Stanford and darting jealous glances at Clive Mawton. Then he'd swallowed a few drinks . . . and now his hostess had palmed him off with this girl, whose hair, a few inches from his nose, smelled pungently of setting lotion. She was a rotten dancer, too . . . after the waltz, he suggested they should go out on to the terrace for some air.

Marion was flattered. She felt it was something to be strolling along the terrace with Tony Welsh. Romantic. There should be a full moon, really. Moon and June. They always went together in the songs. She giggled, partly at this thought, partly from the effects of her second gin-and-lime.

"What's so funny?" Tony asked.

"I was just thinking—there should be a moon to go with it being June, like in the songs."

Tony was amused, but for the wrong reason. "I say, you do that awfully well!" he exclaimed.

"Do what?" Marion was puzzled, and suddenly on her guard.

"Why, that frightful downtown accent! June . . . Moon. You've got it absolutely!"

Marion's superficial feeling of well-being wilted instantly. She felt as crushed as the tawdry pink net of her dance dress. Then she retorted with a surge of defiance: "Is that so? Well, it happens to be the way I speak, *Mr.* Welsh. You see, I come from downtown."

Tony Welsh groaned. This was the last straw. He'd quite thought she was one of his own set, putting on an accent to be amusing. What a ghastly evening! He

supposed he must try to calm her down. "Oh, look here
—don't take umbrage. I didn't mean to hurt your feelings. I'm sorry——" He smiled his most charming smile.
It was quite an effort, but surely it would do the trick.
It usually did. "Come on, let's have a little walk round
the grounds," he went on persuasively. Down to the
rose gardens and back—that would clear his head.

Marion was not charmed by Tony's smile. "Nothing
doing," she exclaimed furiously. "I know what's going
on in your mind. You'd better ask one of your toffee-
nosed girl friends from uptown to go and flirt in the
garden with you instead!"

Then, her feelings thoroughly roused, she slapped
him hard across one side of his face.

Tony winced at the vulgarity of her words, stroked
his cheek tenderly, and gazed after her retreating figure
in dismay. Girls! he thought bitterly. Then he lit a
cigarette and wandered into the garden by himself. He
didn't feel like making a reappearance in public for the
moment, not with five red finger marks across his face.

Suzanne thought it was absurdly romantic to receive
a proposal in a rose garden. Almost as though one were
in the middle of a stage set, with the roses made of
papier-mâché, and she and Gordon two characters in a
drama. Not that this was the first time Gordon had
asked her to marry him; there had been several dress
rehearsals before tonight.

"But why not, Suzanne? Why won't you marry me?"
Gordon Pearce's dejected expression made him look
very young—much younger than his twenty-five years.

"We're so fond of each other, we have the same ideas, we like being together . . ."

Suzanne nervously pleated a fold of her dress between her fingers. She felt sad that she should cause Gordon unhappiness. It was true that she was fond of him, but she knew his fondness for her was the greater. It was not that Suzanne was a romantic; she was aware that many marriages were the more successful because they were founded on companionship, consideration, regard, rather than on a passionate and perishable flame of love. "Fondness" did not seem to her a lukewarm attribute.

She sensed that Gordon, now on the threshold of his career, wanted to tie up the emotional aspect of his life, as it were. After all, she thought with a trace of cynicism, it made life neater to open two ledgers at the same time so that the entries could balance each other: career—marriage; success—family achievement. She was sure Gordon would be successful in his career. He had finished a two-year appointment as House Surgeon at Renchester Infirmary, and had secured a coveted appointment with a London teaching hospital. He would be leaving Renchester very soon. And Suzanne knew she would miss his friendship.

Why shouldn't she accept him, become his wife, help to build both his professional and his family life? She wasn't aware of coherent reasons for rejecting his proposal of marriage; she simply felt instinctively that she wasn't meant to marry him, that her life was to be planned otherwise. Difficult to make Gordon understand this. He was so logical in his outlook. He ex-

pected definite reasons to underlie people's actions. So
she brought out other excuses, knowing she must hurt
him as little as possible.

"It's—it's scarcely the time to think about marriage
. . . children . . . private happiness," she said in a low
voice.

Gordon jerked his head up. "The war, you mean!
Oh, I agree things look black enough. But people have
to get on with their lives just the same. Time doesn't
stand still in times of crisis any more than it does
in the most halcyon days of peace. You can't wait until
the world's like a millpond . . . you might wait forever."

Suzanne gestured with her hands spread palms upwards. "But—bombs—invasion—the Nazi concentration
camps . . . have men and women ever faced such horrors as these?"

"God knows I'm not trying to minimize the horror—
it certainly exists. But I don't believe that at any time
men have felt secure. The threat of the Spanish Armada,
for instance, must have seemed as terrifying at the
time as any invasion plan of Hitler's. The Black Death,
bubonic plague—were they less horrific than poison
gas or high-explosive bombs?" He looked at Suzanne
steadily. "Don't use the certainty of war as an excuse
to save my feelings, Suzanne. You—just don't want to
marry me. It's as simple as that, isn't it?"

Suzanne felt a sudden rush of tears. She nodded
speechlessly.

Gordon stood up, holding out his hands. "Time we
returned to the gay provincial revels," he said. "I
won't bother you any more about this, Suzanne . . .

you know my feelings, and they won't change. If *your* feelings change, let me know."

"Oh, Gordon—I wish I could say Yes. But—I can't."

They walked slowly and sadly back to the house, where the saxophone wailed inexhaustibly.

The End of the Party

Marion had little heart for the gaiety after her encounter with Tony Welsh. In any case it was after twelve; time for Cinderella to be taken home on the back of Ken Martin's motorbike. She found her hostess and said good-by. "A lovely party, Mrs. Mawton—it was ever so kind of you to ask me." Then she felt embarrassed, for it was Mr. Mawton who had asked her, not Mrs. Mawton at all.

But Lily Mawton was kind, and said she hoped Marion had enjoyed herself, and made sure she had someone to see her home.

Marion collected her coat, tied a scarf round her head, and waited in the shadows by the front entrance, where the pillared porch had been newly restored. She hoped Ken would come soon. There were a lot of cars parked in the courtyard before the entrance, gleaming tokens of wealth. Marion wished she were going by car, instead of perching on a motorbike.

At last she heard the roar of Ken's engine as he accelerated up the driveway. If only his bike weren't so noisy! As soon as he stopped, she went over to him.

Ken grinned at her cheerfully. "First time I've known a girl ready and waiting for me! You should tell Evie to take a leaf out of your book—she always keeps me hanging around!" His brash voice rang out, and Marion noticed a group of people by the porch turn to stare at them. "Enjoy the party?" Ken went on. "Hobnobbing with the nobs!" He laughed loudly at his joke.

Marion frowned. "Ssh! Everyone will hear. Don't make so much *noise*."

Ken was annoyed by her tone, but determinedly remained affable, reminding himself that she was Evie's sister. All the same, to have come all this way only to be told to shut up! Who did young Marion think she was?

"O.K., Miss High-and-Mighty, don't worry. I won't disgrace you in front of your new friends."

Marion settled herself on the pillion, wrapping her pink net skirt around her legs. What did it matter now how crushed it got? She'd probably never wear it again, anyway. *She* never went to the Saturday night hops at the local Palais de Danse.

Ken revved up the engine and they set off.

Around midnight, the older guests left the young people still dancing, and retired to the drawing room, where trays of drinks and sandwiches were served as a late supper. Inevitably, the conversation turned to the current topic.

Tobias Clark had sent his wife and two small children off to relatives in America, in the interests of safety. "I can't understand why more people don't do the same," he declared now. "It seems to me the least we can do—

to see our women and children out of the way before
the balloon goes up." He helped himself from a stack
of sandwiches, his fingers fumbling over layers of bread
and ham.

"I should have thought the Royal Family would have
given a lead," he went on. "At least sent the two Princesses across the Atlantic. It wouldn't surprise me to
hear that something has been arranged during this
Canadian tour."

He referred to the Royal tour of Canada and the
United States, from which King George VI and Queen
Elizabeth had just returned.

Henry Mawton looked up.

"That kind of talk sounds very gloomy to me," he
said. "You people take it for granted there's to be a war.
But look at it this way—why should Hitler want war
with Britain? He's succeeded in what he set out to do—
he's restored Germany to a first-class power, he's overrun
Czechoslovakia, he's got Memel for the asking from
Lithuania, he's built up the Axis alliance with Mussolini
. . . he's proved his strength. And he'll stop there, you
mark my words."

He looked round at his guests, who sat silent in the
face of such incredible optimism.

"I'm all for taking a firm stand, mind you," their host
continued. "And I reckon that's just what we've done.
We've called Hitler's bluff by guaranteeing the defense
of Poland, Greece, and Rumania. And don't forget the
British navy—that's the strongest deterrent of all. Germany will think again before pitting herself against our
navy. It doesn't matter how many pocket-battleships and
U-boats she builds, now she's torn up the naval agree-

ment: she hasn't a hope of equaling our naval power."

John Stanford roused himself to say: "Don't forget that our army and air force is far below the strength of the German army and the *Luftwaffe*. If—when—war does come, it will take a superhuman effort to equalize our strengths there."

"Adolf Hitler is a fanatic," Arnold Beaton boomed, in his deep voice, which seemed to give authority to what he said. "Fanatics are never satisfied with what they've achieved. It must be obvious to anyone but a fool that Poland is the next Nazi victim on the list. It's two months since Germany denounced her non-aggression pact with Poland, and now Hitler is massing his troops all along the Polish frontier. It's exactly the same story as Czecho-slovakia last year. And once again, apparently sane people in this country can still blandly assert that those troop movements are merely 'routine autumn maneuvers' for the German army!"

Lily Mawton bridled to hear Arnold Beaton so nearly call her husband a fool. It wasn't in her line to argue about politics, but she felt she must put in a word to support Harry. "Well, all I can say is that I should be very sorry to think we were going to fight the Germans," she said. "We had a very nice young German over from Berlin last year, studying our factory methods. He came over to Parklands quite often in the evenings. About Clive's age, he was. Erich Hoffman—that was his name. Why"—her eyes widened at the thought—"it would be ridiculous to think of our Clive and that German lad as *enemies*."

At this point, the drawing-room door opened and Suzanne slipped in. She had come to find her father, feeling it was time they left the party. Gordon had gone already; he was early duty at the Infirmary this morning. As she entered the room, she heard her father intervene in the conversation. He had sensed Lily Mawton's resentment at Arnold Beaton's tone of voice.

"I'm sure the 'ordinary' people of Germany don't want war with us, any more than we desire war with them. They want to be left in peace, just as we do, to enjoy their family life, their leisure, and to make a success of their work. The way the German crowds acclaimed Chamberlain's peace mission to Munich surely proved that. He received a tremendous ovation. But unfortunately there seem to be two fatal traits in the German character"—he paused, and Suzanne was amused to see that everyone waited for him to continue as though he were about to pronounce upon a dangerous illness— "a desire for power, and admiration for military leadership. The German people appear to me as victims of Nazi aggression no less than the Austrians and the Czechs."

A good diagnosis, Suzanne thought. She moved across the room to perch on the arm of her father's chair. "Time we were off, Father," she whispered in his ear.

Percy Harriman, the master builder, was in the habit of being wise after the event. Whenever the present subject cropped up, he aired an opinion which had now taken on the familiarity of a worn gramophone record.

"We wouldn't be in the dilemma we are today if only all the nations who oppose Nazism had stood together from the beginning—ourselves, America, France, Russia, and the smaller European and Balkan countries. We should have issued a joint declaration that we would all go to the aid of any one member of our pact attacked by Hitler. *That* would have been the really strong line to take. But no—as it is, our only firm ally is France. Russia is a dubious proposition, to say the least. There's even talk of Molotov signing a non-aggression pact with Hitler."

"Percy Harriman proposes a League of Nations as though it were his own original design!" Cynthia Beaton murmured to her husband.

"Still, a League of Nations with the power to act by force of arms if necessary, instead of merely passing recommendations—above all, a League to which America belonged—might have solved all our problems," Arnold Beaton replied.

"France!" Tobias Clark said suddenly. "She may well be thankful for her treaty with us. She gains the protection of the British navy——"

Here Suzanne broke in hotly. She couldn't help herself. The memory of Aunt Clothilde's mingled pride and apprehension during the parade at L'École Militaire, two years ago, flashed through her mind.

"And we gain the protection of the finest army in the world," she declared. "Five million trained men. Do you know what the Nazi propaganda machine is saying to the French? That 'England will fight to the last French soldier.' "

Like everyone else in the room, Tobias Clark remembered that Suzanne Sinclair's mother had been a Frenchwoman. Naturally, she would feel strongly on that score. . . .

John Stanford brought the conversation back into their host's camp. "You seem still to condone the policy of

appeasement we've been following for the last five years,
ever since Hitler came to power," he said to Henry
Mawton. "But can it be condoned—morally? Oh, I
won't pretend I haven't blinded myself to the issues in
recent years. We all have. But my eyes are opened now
all right. This war—*when* it comes—won't be simply a
war of country against country, allies supporting allies.
There's a wider issue. Darkness opposing light, evil
against good, tyranny versus freedom. Think of the Nazi
creed: their inhuman theory of a master race, their persecution of the Jews, their notorious concentration camps,
the way in which Himmler with his Blackshirts has turned
the Kaiser's old secret police into the dreaded Gestapo.
How can anyone who professes to believe in freedom, the
dignity of man, democracy, condone a policy of appeasement with such evil men?"

Margaret Stanford looked anxious as her husband finished his speech. She felt the atmosphere was becoming
strained; the party spirit had definitely departed from
the drawing room. But dance music still sounded from
the library. . . .

Henry Mawton shrugged. "It's always the same story
whenever a dictator comes to power. Dictatorship is
founded on the belief that might is stronger than right,
isn't it? I'm not defending the Nazis—far from it. I
just believe war is avoidable, that's all."

Shortly afterwards, there was a general move home-
wards, and the party dissolved in small talk and fare-
wells. But Percy Harriman's wife paused for a quiet word
with Lily Mawton. The two women were particular
friends.

"I can't help feeling that Harry overdoes his optimism,

Lily," Nancy Harriman remarked. "I have a nasty feeling we warmongers are in the right, you know." Then she added: "Stanley was real disappointed to miss the party. You know he went off to do his military training last week? Trust our Stan to get caught by the first call-up!"

Stanley, her only son, was eighteen.

Lily Mawton pressed her hand. "I sometimes think Harry is trying to convince himself, rather than other people, that there won't be a war," she said. "We missed Stan not being here tonight. If—if it comes, I've an idea Clive will be off into the air force. He's very keen on his weekend flying, you know—it's his latest craze. He was trying to talk Harry into buying a Tiger Moth the other day."

For a moment, something fearful looked out from both women's eyes. It was at though the spirit of Gavin Cortley had returned home to cry aloud: "I died for the light, for the good, for freedom! Who will come after me?"

One advantage of a motorbike, Marion thought, was that you didn't have to carry on a conversation. There was precious little she and Ken Martin had in common to talk about. They roared along the country lanes round Briardale, turned into the new Renchester bypass, then entered the outskirts of the town. In spite of herself, Marion couldn't help but feel exhilarated as the wind streaked past them and they claimed the deserted road for their own with noise and speed.

By the time Ken set her down in Povey Street, outside her own front door, most of her disappointment at

the way the evening had turned out had gone. The parts
she'd enjoyed arranged themselves in the forefront of
her mind.

She tiptoed along the narrow landing to her bedroom,
carrying her dance slippers. Eva's voice called out softly,
and Marion went into her sister's room.

"Well, how did it go? Did you have a good time?"
Eva sat up in bed, her hair pinned in Kirby-grips, traces
of cold cream on her face.

Standing there in the mean little room, with the light
from the gas lamp in the street below shining through
the flimsy cretonne curtains, Marion suddenly thought
longingly of the luxury of Briardale House. There were
thick oyster satin drapes in the bedroom where she'd
left her outdoor things, and a rose-tinted mirror above
the dressing table. . . .

"It was—wonderful," she told Eva simply.

Afterwards, people remembered the Mawtons' housewarming because it was the last really lavish party before
war broke out. That June evening, there were still two
months of uneasy peace ahead before Hitler invaded
Poland on the first day of September, 1939. Peace with
all the signs of war. In the backyards and gardens of
Renchester, air-raid shelters were being hastily erected.
Copies of the Government's A.R.P. handbook, with instructions about stirrup pumps, sandbags, blackout, how
to handle unexploded bombs, lay accessibly in every
house. Gas masks were issued. Every citizen was given
an identity card. And in the cobbled back lanes, in the
school playgrounds, and in the Memorial Recreation

Ground, as they played on the swings, the seesaw, and the roundabout, the children sang a newly minted song:

> *Underneath the spreading chestnut tree,*
> *Mister Chamb'lain said to me:*
> *"If you want to get your gas mask free,*
> *Join the blinking A.R.P.!"*

Opportunity

The Jelinck family was very fond of caraway flavoring.
Caraway bread, caraway cake, and especially caraway
dumplings in soup. But it didn't seem possible to buy
caraway seeds in Renchester. Antonia Jelinck was not
sure whether this was really so, or whether it was her
shaky grasp of the English language that puzzled the
shopkeepers. So when, at breakfast one October morning,
Anna asked if they could have dumplings in soup for
supper that evening, her mother replied:

"Certainly we shall have dumplings. And if your father
can find some caraway seeds during his travels today,
they shall be caraway dumplings."

"The Golem's dumplings!" Anna cried.

That was what they were called back home in Prague.
There was a legend about the Golem, a magic creature
that was supposed to have been created by a rabbi who
had once lived in the narrow twisting Street of the
Alchemists, in the oldest part of the city. The Golem

escaped from his master, and ran about the streets spreading terror until the rabbi snatched from its mouth a piece of paper bearing the magic signs which had brought it to life—whereupon it fell dead at his feet. There were some rags preserved in the old synagogue which were supposed to have been the Golem's coat. Anna remembered how she and Tomas had gazed at them wonderingly, half believing and half distrusting the legend. She didn't know why caraway dumplings were called the Golem's dumplings. Maybe the creature had lived on them. But, as Tomas had pointed out, how could it eat with the magic paper in its mouth?

Anna had a sudden vivid memory of Tomas's teasing voice. She bent her head over her bowl of milky coffee. If only memories of him would not come so unexpectedly. . . .

Josef Jelinck got up from the table. It was time for him to set out for work.

"In the High Street there is a big grocery store, nearby Mr. Prendergast's shop," he said. "There I will go. In so large an establishment there will surely be one little packet of caraway seeds."

He consulted a typewritten sheet of names and addresses, the list of his day's calls. He could not pretend his heart was in his new work as a piano tuner and repairer for Mr. Prendergast, but it had a certain interest of its own. First on the list today was number 8, Laburnum Close, just around the corner. Then he must take a tram ride downtown to Milton Road Council School, to look at the piano in the assembly hall there. After that, there was a visit to Miss Iris Maloney, who gave private piano lessons; a call at the Marina Dance

Hall; and then a booking for a Mr. Seton, who lived in
Alban Road, in the seedy area of the town behind the
Infirmary.

"Come, Anna, you must not be late for school."

Her mother hustled her into her navy-blue coat and
carefully smoothed her velour hat with its green-and-
white High School ribbon. Anna pulled the hat over
her dark hair, and picked up her satchel and her gas
mask in its cardboard box.

The overcoat and velour hat were the only proper
items of High School uniform she possessed, and it had
been difficult to afford even these. For the rest, her
mother had devised a navy-blue tunic out of an alpaca
dress of her own, and had bought two cheap, badly cut
blouses at a little shop downtown. You were supposed
to buy all your uniform at Burridge's. Anna wished her
blouses were like those of the other girls, but she knew
they were much too expensive. She wished, too, that she
had a nice leather case to carry her gas mask in, but such
a luxury was out of the question.

Anna and her father left the house in Derwent Crescent
together. It was a clear day; above them in a blue sky
barrage balloons floated like imitation silver clouds. In
spite of the barrage balloons, in spite of the square cardboard box slung over Anna's shoulders, the war seemed
very far away that morning. Impossible to imagine dark
waves of Nazi bombers cutting through that blue English
sky! The Anderson shelters, the garden trenches, the strips
of paper pasted across the windows of the houses as a protection against blast, seemed unnecessary precautions. As
yet there had been no sign of the *Luftwaffe's* threatened

attacks on Britain. The glorious summer of 1939 was declining peacefully into autumn.

It was over a month now since Mr. Chamberlain's broadcast announcement, on September 3, that Great Britain was at war with Germany. In mid-September, British soldiers had been sent to France to reinforce the French army. Meanwhile, the Nazi invasion of Poland had been completed; after holding out for ten days, Warsaw had surrendered on September 27.

Josef Jelinck turned off into Laburnum Close, and Anna went on to the bus stop alone, swinging her satchel and thinking how safe, how secure it felt to be living in this suburb of little houses surrounded by creosoted fences and orderly gardens. She liked Renchester much better than London. In London, they had lived in two rooms in a Soho street. Her father had played in a "Bohemian" café orchestra, wearing a ridiculous fancy dress of baggy satin trousers, full-sleeved shirt, and velvet bolero. Her mother had been employed in the same café as a waitress. It was an unhappy time. Then, just when things got worse than ever, when her father's arm had become so bad that he couldn't play the violin any longer, they had heard from the Refugee Organization. Now they had a chance to begin again. They were the Jelinck family of Derwent Crescent, Renchester. The Jelincks of Mala Strana, Prague, did not exist any more.

At the High School, Anna had made particular friends with two other girls in her form, Flora Stanford and Janet Murdoch. She and Janet were invited for tea at Flora's house today. Janet had told Anna that the Stanfords were rich, and had a "posh" house. (Anna

wasn't quite sure what this word *posh* meant.) The
Murdochs lived in a house in Oakdene Gardens, quite
near Derwent Crescent. Janet was a lively girl, always
getting into some scrape or other at school. Last week
she had screwed off the handle inside the form-room
door so that Miss Cochran wouldn't be able to get in
to give them a history lesson. Unfortunately for Janet,
however, it was not Miss Cochran who came along; she
was away that day, and the headmistress herself had
decided to give Upper III their history lesson. . . .

Last Saturday afternoon, Anna, Flora, and Janet had
seen a film at the Granada—*The Little Princess*. It was all
about a Victorian girl called Sarah Crewe, who was left
in a boarding school in London when her father went
to India. At first everything was splendid: Sarah was
treated kindly, and wore lovely clothes. Then the money
her father had left ran out, and there was no word from
him; it was supposed he was dead. Sarah became a
drudge at the school, and had to carry coals up long
flights of stairs. However, it all came right in the end.
Her father returned home, and Sarah wore her lovely
clothes again. The three girls had all cried over the sad
parts in the film, and afterwards Flora had lent Anna
another story by the author of *The Little Princess*. It was
called *The Secret Garden*. At home, in the apartment on
the Mala Strana, Anna had shelves filled with books
in her bedroom, but of course they were all left behind
that dreadful night when they had escaped. . . . What
had happened to the books, and to her collection of glass
animals, and all their other possessions? Perhaps some
German officer was living in their apartment now,

enjoying the splendid view of the river Vltava from the wide window of the sitting room. . . .

Suddenly she thought of Tomas again, and the book of poems he had given her for her last birthday. If only she could have brought that one book to England! Standing at the bus stop, she shuddered as she remembered how Andreas Losha, a fellow student of Tomas's, had rushed into the apartment to tell them that Tomas had been rounded up with a group of other University students, and marched off by SS guards. The Gestapo! Their ruthlessness far outstripped the legendary terror of the Golem. . . . No one knew what had happened to the students, whether they had been shot, or deported to Germany, either to a concentration camp, or to join the Nazi forced-labor units. Perhaps, Anna thought, perhaps Tomas would come back when the war was over and the Germans were defeated, when Czechoslovakia was free once more. Just as Sarah Crewe's father had come back at the end of the story. Was it too much to hope for?

The bus, a number 5, with *All Saints* on the destination board, arrived. Anna climbed the stairs. Janet boarded the bus two stops earlier, and always sat in one of the front seats on the top deck. Yes, there she was, looking round for Anna, her school hat crammed down on her fair hair. . . .

"Mournfully the old ghosts wander from room to room. Mournfully the old ghosts wander . . ."

There was a shout of laughter. Marion swiveled round in her typing chair, nearly swallowing the little ivory wedge she held between her front teeth. Hastily she removed it and glared at Geoff Chanter, who stood in the doorway of the office.

"What on earth are you doing?" Geoff asked, recovering from his amusement. "Going to give a recitation at the church concert?" He collapsed into laughter again.

"If you must know," Marion said icily, "I'm practicing my speech-training exercises."

"So that's it!" Geoff came over and perched on the corner of her desk. "It's the 'how now brown cow' routine, is it? I must say I've been wondering what's come over your voice lately. You've been sounding as though you had a mouthful of plums every time you said anything."

"And what makes you think I'm the slightest bit interested in *your* opinion of my voice, Geoff Chanter?"

Marion looked and sounded really annoyed, and Geoff suddenly stopped being amused.

"You know, your trouble is that you take yourself too seriously, my girl. So you're having speech training, are you?" He chuckled again. "You'll be having your face lifted next!"

"Why shouldn't I improve my voice if I want to? I don't want to be stuck with a Renchester accent all my life."

Geoff shrugged. "Personally, I'm glad I've got a bit of an accent. Gives your voice some character, if you ask me. It'd be pretty dull if everyone went around talking BBC. No, you may be trying to change your voice, Marion, but in my opinion you won't improve it."

"I've told you already, I'm not interested in your opinion."

Marion noted crossly that her Renchester accent became more pronounced when she was annoyed. Still, she'd only had four lessons so far. The whole course lasted three months; by the end of that time she was determined to have said good-by to every trace of "that frightful downtown accent."

The memory of the incident with Tony Welsh had remained with her, irritating as a wrinkled sock inside a shoe. Then she had gone to see *Pygmalion* at the Eldorado, with Wendy Hiller as Eliza Dolittle. Eliza's struggles with "the rain in Spain" had first put into Marion's mind the idea of having *her* voice trained. It seemed an extraordinary coincidence (though in fact the advertisement appeared in the *Echo* each week) when, the very day after seeing the film, she'd seen this notice in the local paper: *Miss Iris Maloney. Piano lessons. Speech training*.

Marion had begun her course the next week; already her native accent was being submerged beneath a refinement of vowels and a clipping of consonants. Practicing the exercises was a problem. She hadn't told her family about the course—she was afraid of their ridicule. As it was, they had commented on her changing voice. Her mother had asked if she had a sore throat; her father had accused her of being "la-di-da"; Eva was always asking her to repeat remarks. It was impossible to practice her exercises aloud at home; anything you said could be heard all over the little Povey Street house. The only thing was to practice in the office, in her lunch hour. Until today, she had managed to finish the exercises before Geoff returned. (Recently he'd received a raise in salary, and as a

result always went out for lunch. Bloater-paste sandwiches were a thing of the past.)

Now Geoff grinned at Marion. "In that case," he
said, in answer to her last remark, "you'll be glad to
know that you won't have to listen to my opinions much
longer. In fact, you'll most likely have this desirable,
semi-detached, glass-partitioned rabbit hutch all to yourself—for I doubt if Mr. Stanford will bother to replace
me. Business isn't exactly booming these days, and this
is not a reserved occupation."

Marion stared at him. "What d'you mean?"

"I mean that I got my call-up papers this morning.
Buff envelope. 'On His Majesty's Service.' Into the army
I go. Private Chanter, that's me." He gave a mock salute,
then laughed at the expression on Marion's face. "It's
not really so surprising, you know! All we healthy young
lads are off to fight the war . . . hadn't you noticed?"

Marion had noticed. Most of the young men round
about Povey Street had gone into khaki, air-force blue,
or bell-bottomed trousers. Ken Martin had joined the
army; Eva spent Saturday nights alone these days.

"I'll—I'll miss you, Geoff," Marion said lamely. What
else could she say?

"Like heck you will!" Geoff had no illusions about
their relationship. He began opening all the drawers in
his desk, sorting out rubbish. "Might as well do this
now," he remarked. "All I've got on this afternoon is a
rent-collection job." He brought out a bar of nut milk
chocolate from the back of one of the drawers. "Here—
have half to celebrate my retirement from Stanford &
Earle, Limited." He placed a pile of books on top of the
desk. "These are my textbooks for the Chartered Auc-

tioneers' exams. Doesn't look as though I'll be needing them for some time—might as well leave them here, I suppose."

Later that afternoon, when Geoff had gone out rent-collecting, Marion found herself with no work on hand. There were few sale particulars to type out and duplicate these days. Idly she picked up one of the books on Geoff's desk, and examined the contents.

Then she began turning the pages with more definite interest. Ambition stirred in her. Women as well as men could take these exams, gain the qualifications for which Geoff had been studying. *Why shouldn't she?* If Mr. Stanford didn't engage another clerk instead of Geoff, she might get the chance of doing some of Geoff's work. Then, if she proved herself capable, Mr. Stanford might let her take over his job completely. And if, in the meantime, she studied for these exams . . . Why, this was her chance, the chance she had always hoped would come her way! Her opportunity to prove herself! She knew she must seize it with both hands.

A Friend Well Met

Josef Jelinck came out of the grocer's in the High Street in triumph, bearing a packet of caraway seeds. Antonia would be pleased, and Anna should have her dumplings for supper. He beamed with pleasure as he walked along in the direction of the Infirmary.

On the whole it had been a good day. His first call, however, in Laburnum Close, hadn't been very satisfactory. A rosy-cheeked maid had admitted him to an over-furnished lounge: embroidered antimacassars on the settee and easy chairs, lace runners on the little tables, a loudly patterned carpet, an upright piano of inferior make. Then the mistress of the house had appeared, and surveyed him suspiciously. "A foreigner!" Josef read her thought as she heard his accent.

"The piano only needs tuning," she told him authoritatively.

He'd noticed some books of elementary exercises: *First Pianoforte Lessons*.

"My little girl plays," the woman had told him, indicating a framed photograph of a child with Shirley Temple curls and freckles.

He had tuned the piano as quickly as possible, aware that the rosy-cheeked maid had been instructed to "keep an eye on him—just in case." The lounge door was left open and she hovered in the hall, leaning on a carpet sweeper.

That had been a dull visit. But the subsequent calls at Milton Road School and Miss Maloney's house had passed off pleasantly, and after lunch he had repaired a string in the piano at the Marina Dance Hall.

"He's done it again!" the caretaker had greeted Josef as he let him into the hall. "Mr. Lewis is always warnin' 'im about 'itting the keys so 'ard."

"He" was the pianist in Benny Lewis's band, which played at the Marina three nights a week.

And now, after his successful visit to the grocer's, Josef was on his way to Mr. Seton, his last call of the day.

He reached Alban Road. It was typical of those east-end streets of slums. Lately, however, a change had come upon this sleazy neighborhood. Children no longer ran shrieking up and down the pavements, or rattled along the roads in orange-box bogies. It was as though the Pied Piper had strolled by. In fact, with gas masks hung round their necks and identification labels tied to the buttonholes of their coats, the children had been evacuated to the safety of the surrounding countryside. The shrill-voiced, black-shawled women who used to cluster like crows on the unscrubbed steps of the houses had largely disappeared, too. Now, wearing scarves wrapped turban-wise round their heads, they went out to work in the downtown factories, taking the places of the men who had been called up. Only the old men were left to congregate on the street corners, hang around the public houses till opening time, and make their regular expeditions to draw the dole.

The houses, lacking the old liveliness and noise that used to surround them, looked more squalid than ever. Josef was depressed by the broken railings, peeling paint, and gaping doors. He walked along looking for Mr. Seton's house. Then he stopped. This was it. He stood for a moment outside the gate. There was something different about this house. A secret, shuttered atmosphere. Its life did not spill out and merge with the street. Dingy lace curtains screened the closed windows. The front door was shut—a phenomenon in this road of shared living quarters.

He walked up the path, flanked on either side by an unkempt privet hedge. There was a brass plate beside the door, inscribed in the old-fashioned provincial manner with the householder's name: *Theodore Seton, Esq.* Josef pulled the bell and heard it jangling inside the hall. After an interval there was a shuffling of slippered feet, a bolt was undrawn, and the door was opened cautiously.

Josef found himself face to face with a frail, elderly man wearing a velvet jacket, ancient black trousers, and checked carpet slippers. His face and chin were covered in silver-gray stubble. Yet he had a curious dignity, and when Josef announced himself, he bade him enter with a gracious air.

The hall was gloomy, filled with heavy mahogany furniture. A thick layer of dust covered everything. Mr.

Seton led the way upstairs into a large back room. At first glance this room seemed to contain an extraordinary assortment of things, but as Josef looked more closely around him, he realized that the old man had gathered here all the necessities of his life.

A brass-knobbed bedstead and a wardrobe stood in one corner. In the middle of the room was a large table, half its surface covered with a cloth and bearing the remains of a frugal meal. A wireless set occupied the other half of the table. Shelves filled with books and bound volumes of old magazines stretched along one wall. A small cooking stove stood beside a sink, and a comfortable armchair was drawn up before the gas fire. There were prints and engravings in gilt frames on every wall. But the room was dominated by the piano, a Bechstein grand, which stood between the two windows of the room, framed by their heavy plush curtains. In contrast to the other furniture, the piano shone with polish, and the ivory keys gleamed whitely. Sheet music and portfolios were piled in heaps on the floor.

The old man waved one hand around the room. "I don't use the rest of the house," he said. "The other rooms have been shut up for years. People wonder why I remain here. But this house has always been my home. Here I was born, here I shall die. I daresay you noticed the brass plate at the door. Theodore Seton was my father." Then he indicated the Bechstein. "This is my piano, Mr. Jelinck. I have it tuned three or four times each year."

Josef was oddly pleased that this old man had remembered his name and pronounced it correctly. Usually, he found, English people could neither remember

it nor twist their tongues around the unaccustomed pro-
nunciation of the J as Y.

"You play a good deal?" he asked, going over to the
piano with his tuning fork.

"Every day," Mr. Seton replied. "The piano is my only
joy in life."

Josef was puzzled, but did not like to probe further.
He got on with his job, and meanwhile the old man put
a kettle of water to boil on the stove, and produced a
teapot, a bottle of milk, and two cups.

While he was drinking his tea, Josef's glance fell upon
a photograph that stood in the middle of the mantel. It
showed three young men with linked arms, their caps
tilted back on their heads, laughing at whoever had held
the camera. Suddenly Josef leaned forward; he thought
he recognized one of the young men. . . .

"Surely," he said, "that young man in the middle . . . ?"

Mr. Seton smiled. "Yes," he replied, "it is Jan Paderewski. We were students together in Vienna. Leschetizky
was our master. The third lad was another student—also
a Pole, like Jan. What patriotic sentiments he and Jan
indulged in!" He sighed. "I have been thinking a good
deal lately of those two fellow students of mine. Especially of Jan Paderewski. How bitterly he must have
felt the German invasion of Poland, after he worked so
hard and so long for the independence of his country."

"I think he must be the only professional musician ever
to have become Prime Minister of his country," Josef
remarked. "He is living now in New York, is he not?"

"Yes, that's so. We lost touch with one another a long
time ago. He is a very great pianist; I am a failure. Oh,

yes"—he waved one hand in a self-deprecating gesture—
"I have no illusions about myself, about my ability as a
pianist. But none the less, music, the piano, remains my
joy in life."

Josef was fascinated by the old man. To have found an
ex-pupil of Leschetizky, a fellow student of Paderewski,
in this seedy street here in Renchester! As he lingered
over his tea, Aubrey Seton described to him his unsuccessful debut in London, in the 1890s, and how afterwards
he had abandoned all thought of a career as a concert
pianist, and retired to this house, living quietly with
music as the background to his existence.

"I see few people nowadays," he finished. "Most of
my friends are gone away. There used to be a music
society in Renchester, but that too is no more."

The two men stayed talking until it was time to blackout the windows and light the gas mantles. Josef told
Aubrey Seton his own story, and related his memory of
an occasion when Jan Paderewski had come to Prague
to take part in a concert with the Conservatoire Orchestra.
When he left the house in Alban Road, it was with the
promise that he would return soon—not as Mr. Prendergast's piano tuner, but as a friend.

Anna knew now what Janet had meant when she described the Stanfords' house as "posh." She was impressed
by the secluded atmosphere and quiet, graveled roads
of Parklands. The horse-chestnut trees, their foliage au-
tumn-colored, bore glossy brown conkers in green, spiky
cases. Only one house looked out of place to Anna. It
stood empty on the corner by the pillar box. Its windows

stared blankly; the grass of the front lawn had grown knee high, and sprouted untidily through the fence with its peeling white paint.

"Daddy says that house will probably stay empty for the duration," Flora remarked as they passed by. "It used to belong to some people called Mawton. Clive Mawton is my sister's boy friend. He's a pilot in the RAF. There's a super cherry tree in the back garden. Whitehearts. I pinched lots from it in the summer!"

After tea, the three girls went up to Flora's room and discussed the day's great topic of school news. Miss Sinclair was leaving! This had been announced after prayers, the customary time for giving out notices, reading the lost-property lists, and announcing the results of game fixtures. By now, Anna had grown used to the extraordinary passion these English schoolgirls showed for playing netball, hockey, tennis . . .

"I know we shall all regret Miss Sinclair's departure," the headmistress had remarked. This was what she always said when any member of staff left the school, and in this case it was quite true. Miss Sinclair was one of the most popular mistresses; Flora was not the only girl who had a "crush" on her.

At first, everyone had speculated on whether she was leaving to get married, but evidently this was not so.

"I wonder what other school she's going to," Flora said dejectedly, sitting on the chintz-covered window seat.

Janet, who was sprawled on the divan bed, suddenly looked important. "She's not going to another school. She's giving up teaching."

"What! How do you know? What's she going to do, then?"

"She's going to work in London—at the Foreign Office, or the War Office, or something." Janet was vague about the exact details. "I know, because my cousin's in the Upper Fifth, and Miss Sinclair's her form-mistress. She told them about it this morning."

"London!" Flora exclaimed. "I expect she's going to do some frightfully important job." Somehow, she felt cheered by this news; it had been awful to think of losing Miss Sinclair to unknown girls at another school.

"I like Miss Sinclair," Anna said. "She is young and gay. I too am sorry she is leaving."

But Anna could not really understand how Flora could have a "crush" on their French mistress. This was something else about her new English school she thought strange. There had been both boys and girls at the school where she had been a pupil in Prague, and men and women teachers. Quite often the girls had had "crushes" on the boys, or the men teachers—that seemed logical. Anna herself had admired the young history professor. How happy she used to feel when he gave her good marks for her essays! Her father had told her that the Germans had introduced a new sort of history in Czech schools and universities now. Everyone had to learn history from the Nazi point of view, which taught that Germany was the world's master race. Anna was sure that the young history professor would never have agreed to teach this sort of history. She wondered what had happened to him. Had he suffered the same fate as Tomas—whatever that might be?

"Well, I think Miss Sinclair is jolly sensible to stop being a teacher," Janet said definitely. "It's such a dreary thing to be. Look at the rest of the staff—what frumps!

You can *tell* they're schoolteachers a mile off. It's the last thing I'll be when I leave school!"

"It's about the only career you haven't decided on at one time or another," Flora teased her.

Janet was always choosing her future career. So far this had varied from helping to run a riding school, being a veterinary surgeon, becoming a famous air woman like Jean Batten or Amy Mollison, and taking up journalism.

Anna was looking at Flora's collection of glass ornaments, arranged on a shelf by her bed. They reminded her of the collection she had left behind at home. One little orange tree in particular, with fragile, transparent glass leaves . . . surely it was the same as one she used to have! She turned it upside down. Yes—there were the words "Made in Czechoslovakia" printed on a label stuck to the base. When she told Flora this, to her embarrassment Flora insisted on giving her the little tree.

"You must take it," she urged generously. "It can be the beginning of your new collection."

"How awful to have lost all your other things," Janet exclaimed.

The loss of Anna's collection of glass ornaments, trivial enough in itself, seemed to bring home to the two English girls a vivid realization of the tragedy of the refugee.

Shortly after six, Janet and Anna left for home. When they went to say good-by to Flora's mother, they found her listening to the six o'clock news on the wireless. These days, every news program had assumed vital importance. Tonight, Mrs. Stanford's face was grave.

"There's bad news," she told the three girls. "One of our battleships, *The Royal Oak,* has been sunk by a German submarine at Scapa Flow. There are very few survivors; the ship capsized and sank in a few moments."

"But—Scapa Flow!" Flora exclaimed. "That's in Scotland, in the Orkneys, isn't it?"

Her mother nodded. "Our entire Home Fleet is based there. Apparently the U-boat sneaked through our defenses, fired its torpedoes, and made off again without being detected. It's terrible to think of that huge battleship, with hundreds of men on board, sinking in such an incredibly short time."

She reminded Flora to turn out the hall light before opening the front door. Percy Harriman, who had become their local air-raid warden, was very particular about the slightest glimmer of light showing from any of the Parklands houses.

Anna and Janet didn't talk much on their way home in the bus. The blackout, the unlit street lamps, dark houses, the masked headlights of cars—all these made the October evening seem unusually dark. What a contrast it was to the blue skies of that morning, Anna thought. She arrived home to find her mother busy at the kitchen table, working the dough for their dumplings. A large pan of onion soup was simmering on the stove.

Antonia Jelinck beamed happily at her daughter, and wiped her floury hands on her apron. "Your papa came home with the caraway seeds!" she greeted Anna. "Tonight we shall have a supper just like the old days."

Anna sniffed the good onion smell appreciatively, and began grating a bowlful of cheese to sprinkle over the soup.

"Tonight your papa is glad in his heart," her mother continued. "He has met a friend, a good old man who has studied music in Vienna."

"That is good. I am happy for him." Anna knew that her father often felt lonely. He used to have so many friends back home.

She laid the supper table with a blue-and-white checked cloth and the Woolworth cutlery they had bought in London. Beside each place she put one of her mother's crisp, home-baked rolls. Then, as a final touch, to celebrate the Golem's dumplings, she placed the little glass orange tree in the center of the table.

Family Group

The queue for the ninepennies stretched right round the corner of the Odeon. It was half past seven, an evening in early May; dusk was just turning to darkness. Ken and Eva stood together towards the back of the queue. They were waiting to see Fred Astaire and Ginger Rogers in *The Story of Vernon and Irene Castle.* Their choice had lain between this or *The Four Feathers,* at the Eldorado; they had decided Fred Astaire and Ginger Rogers offered gayer entertainment. Eva badly needed cheering up; Ken was on ten days' embarkation leave before his unit left for France.

Ken lit another cigarette from the butt of the one he'd just finished. The tip glowed red in the dusk as he drew on it. He didn't usually chain smoke, but for the last half hour or so, ever since they'd joined the queue, he had been trying to find words for what was to be the most important speech in his life to date.

Eva rested against his arm, wishing she had put on

more comfortable shoes. Still, she could kick these off once they got inside the cinema. She only hoped they'd get seats and wouldn't have to stand. But even if they did have to stand, it was lovely to be going to the pictures again with Ken. It seemed ages since the days when they used to go out either to a film or else to the Palais every Saturday night. Funny how your life could change so much. It had all seemed so safe before, as though nothing would ever upset it—why, at times she'd even felt those regular Saturday night outings were monotonous! Then suddenly this war had come, and here they were: Ken in khaki battledress, and she herself looking forward to the film as though it were her very first visit to the cinema with him.

"Evie," Ken said suddenly, "let's get married."

Eva gasped. "Oh, Ken——"

"I mean now," Ken said. "Before my leave's up. It'll mean a special license . . . what about it, Evie?"

Eva had always known she and Ken would get married one day, of course. Everyone knew they were going steady. But she had never thought it would happen like this. If it hadn't been wartime, if Ken still had his job at the garage, they would have waited until he was earning a better wage, until they had saved up enough to put down a deposit on a little house . . . one of those bungalows on the new housing estates, right away from the Povey Street area. It was so clean and fresh up there; Ken used to take her there on the back of his motorbike Sunday afternoons, and they'd daydream about a place of their own. . . .

But it *was* wartime, and Ken was no longer at the garage. And, somehow, considerations about saving money to buy red-brick bungalows and the furniture to go inside them didn't seem to matter any more. Now it was a question of deciding either to marry the person you loved, or to face the possibility of losing that chance forever. Eva knew what she wanted. She wanted to marry Ken, even if their marriage was destined to last only a few weeks.

They were two anonymous people in a cinema queue; nobody cared, few even noticed, when Ken put his arms round Eva and kissed her after she told him this.

"Evie," he said, "special licenses cost quite a bit—I shan't be able to afford an engagement ring as well. But I got you this instead." He fumbled in a pocket of his battledress, and brought out a little cardboard box. Inside was a brooch, two hearts entwined in the center of a rolled-gold bar.

Eva brushed one hand across her eyes. "It's—it's lovely, Ken." She took the brooch out of the box and pinned it on the lapel of her coat, then looked up at him with shining eyes.

The queue shuffled a few yards towards the cinema entrance, and they found themselves standing beside a display of photographs advertising next week's film. Ken glanced at these, then looked at Eva.

"Norma Shearer isn't a patch on you, Evie," he told her.

A few moments later, it began to rain. Umbrellas sprouted among the queue like mushrooms. Eva brought at oil-silk pixie hood out of her handbag and put it on her head. Ken suddenly took her arm.

"Come on," he said, "this is a special evening. We're going in the three bobs!"

So they walked right past the ninepenny queue, straight

into the cinema, and found two vacant places in the three-shilling seats, in the front rows of the circle upstairs—the best seats in the house. A newsreel was in progress as they settled down in the comfort of plush and warmth. Eva kicked off her shoes with relief, and Ken put an arm around her shoulders.

The screen showed pictures of the ill-fated campaign in Norway, where British and French forces were retreating before the German invader. The cinema audience sat silently. There was a good deal of criticism directed against the Conservative Government at the moment, and talk of the Norwegian campaign having been mismanaged. From the first, ever since the Allied troops landed in Trondheim following the Nazi invasion of Denmark and Norway early in April, they had fought a losing battle. The Germans were now in complete control of Denmark and all but a small area of Norway. There were plenty of people who thought Neville Chamberlain should resign as Prime Minister, and that a new Government, a coalition of the best politicians in every party, should be formed under a different leader. Party politics were of little account now; patriotism and individual qualities of leadership took pride of place.

After the newsreel, there was an interlude. The lights went up and the cinema organist played popular tunes while the audience joined in singing. Most of the singing came from the cheaper seats; the people in the circle didn't seem to enjoy taking part. Eva and Ken discussed their wedding plans to the accompaniment of "Roll Out the Barrel."

"Mum will be disappointed we're not getting married

in church," Eva said. "She doesn't hold with registry office weddings."

Ken looked alarmed. "Not changing your mind, love?"

The organist twiddled a group of notes as he came to the end of "Roll Out the Barrel," and then launched into "We're Going to Hang Out the Washing on the Siegfried Line."

Eva smiled, and squeezed Ken's arm. "Course not. It's our wedding, not hers."

"We're going to *hang* out the washing on the *Sieg*fried Line . . ."

They made plans for a three-day honeymoon in London. Ken knew of a hotel near King's Cross where they could stay. He'd visited London once before, to see a Cup Final at Wembley when Renchester United had been in the First Division.

The ninepenny chorus sang lustily:

"We're going to *hang* out the washing on the *Sieg*fried Line. . . .

If the *Sieg*fried Line's still there!"

Eva decided she would buy a new spring costume for her trousseau, and a smart hat. She'd wear a flower in her jacket for the wedding—a gardenia, perhaps. She didn't care much for carnations, they had such a sickly scent. When the main film began, she nestled her head on Ken's shoulder and sighed contentedly. Fred Astaire and Ginger Rogers danced their way through the story of Vernon and Irene Castle, and Eva Gray thought she had never felt so happy in her life.

Marion had no difficulty in getting the morning off to attend Eva's wedding the following week. Ever since

Geoff Chanter had gone into the army, Mr. Stanford
had been giving Marion increasingly responsible jobs.
In fact, Marion was fast becoming indispensable to Stanford & Earle, and her employer was anxious not to give
her any cause for dissatisfaction. She had already received
a raise in pay, and Mr. Stanford was encouraging when
she told him she was thinking of studying for the Chartered Auctioneers' exams.

Eva and Ken were married in the registrar's office at
the Town Hall. Afterwards there was to be a lunch party
at Burridge's restaurant. Besides the two families, a girl
friend of Eva's was included in the party, and a friend
of Ken's called Joe. Joe was president of the Renchester
Motor Cycle Club.

Ken's parents had reacted to the suddenness of this
wedding more easily than Eva's.

"It's not like a proper wedding at all," Mrs. Gray remarked sadly to Marion, as they stood waiting for the
registrar.

"Cheer up, Mother," Marion replied. (Nowadays she
never called her mother "Mum," as she used to.) "At
least there's a vase of flowers on the table."

But the orange-eye narcissi in the green pottery vase
didn't console Mrs. Gray.

"I did want both you girls to have real nice weddings,"
she sighed. "There's nothing nicer than a nice wedding,
with everything done proper."

Into her mind's eye came a picture of Eva's wedding as
she would have liked it to be: the ceremony at St. Mark's,
the Victorian chapel at the corner of Povey Street; Eva
in a white satin dress with a tulle veil, Ken in a smart
lounge suit with a carnation in his buttonhole; photo-

graphs taken outside the chapel afterwards; a party in the church hall, with a three-tiered wedding cake and someone making a humorous speech . . .

The reality was so different. Here was Eva, wearing an ordinary blue costume with a pink lace blouse, and a little straw hat perched on top of her head. Ken was in uniform, of course. No orange blossom, no floating tulle, no bouquets . . .

Marion shrugged in response to her mother's complaint. She had no fixed ideas about weddings; she never window-shopped for bridal dresses. She couldn't really understand what Eva saw in Ken Martin, or why they had decided to get married now, but that was Eva's business. So far as Marion could see, her sister's life would be changed very little by the fact that she was Mrs. Ken Martin. She was to go on living at home while Ken was away, and was keeping on her job at the hairdressing salon.

Eva's father had no very definite views on the marriage —though he had half-heartedly expressed the opinion that Ken wasn't really "good enough" for his daughter. But his thoughts just now were much more concerned with the progress of the war than any wedding. His opinion of the Tories' handling of the war to date was much stronger than his views of Ken's eligibility. He thoroughly sympathized with Herbert Morrison's attack on the Government in the House of Commons a few days ago—as a result of which Mr. Chamberlain had asked the House for a vote of confidence, and the Government's majority had fallen to eighty-one. Two days later, Neville Chamberlain had resigned; Winston Churchill (a Tory, it was true, but a Tory with a rebel's reputation) had formed the Coalition Government. And not a day too soon, in Mr. Gray's opinion. The change of Government coincided with Hitler's invasion of Holland and Belgium: there was heavy fighting along the Meuse; the Germans were pressing westward behind the French defenses.

Suddenly the war seemed much nearer home; now Ken's imminent departure for France meant a departure into battle. . . .

There was a pause outside the Town Hall after the ceremony was over. Ken's father had managed to obtain a roll of film (like so many other things, film had become very scarce nowadays) and had brought along his camera. After snapping Ken and Eva standing arm-in-arm on the steps, he spent a long time grouping the rest of the party within the range of his lens.

Mrs. Gray faced the camera with a set smile; in her opinion, a photograph on the Town Hall steps was a poor substitute for one in the porch of St. Mark's. Ken's mother was feeling tearful; she liked Eva and was happy about the marriage, but Ken was joining his unit immediately after the brief honeymoon in London, and she wouldn't see him again until his next leave, whenever that might be. Mr. Gray fidgeted in front of the camera (later his face came out blurred on the print). He was feeling peckish, and wanted his dinner.

Marion felt conspicuous, standing there in front of the Town Hall with people passing by all the time. She wished Ken's father would hurry up. Just as she thought he had finished, he handed her the camera and asked her to take a group that included himself. She fiddled with the view finder, then looked up to warn everyone she was about to take the photo. And, quite suddenly, an intense feeling of emotion seized her by the throat. Eva looked so extraordinarily happy, Ken so filled with pride, as they stood together on the grimy stone steps, flanked by walls of anti-blast sandbags built around the entrance to the Town Hall. And they both looked so young. . . . It was a curious thing, but at that moment Marion felt much older than her elder sister. Her eyes filled with tears, and the image of the family group swam before her as the camera clicked.

"Oh, look—how sweet. They've just been married!"

Pauline leaned across the table to touch Clive's sleeve and direct his attention to the wedding party that had just entered the restaurant.

Clive glanced over his shoulder. "Wartime weddings always seem more romantic," he observed, taking in the young, khaki-clad bridegroom. Then he grinned. "Like to try one?"

Pauline smiled enigmatically. She was almost sure he was joking.

The girl who had been married wore a bright blue suit with a gardenia in one lapel, and a little hat tilted over one eye. The party obviously belonged downtown. They seemed a bit overawed by their surroundings at first, but after a whispered consultation, someone at the table ordered champagne, and they soon relaxed and began talking and laughing.

"Hallo, I believe the rather serious-looking girl who looks a bit like the bride works in Daddy's office,"

Pauline said, continuing to dart glances at their table. "She's called Miriam—or is it Marion? I forget. Anyway, according to Daddy, she's quite a career girl."

"Really?" Clive didn't share Pauline's interest in the wedding party. He'd been in the middle of an amusing story about his wing commander when they came in. He tried to pick up the thread of the story, but there didn't seem to be so much point to it now.

Clive was enjoying life in the air force. He was stationed with a Hurricane fighter squadron in the south of England. He enjoyed the easy comradeship of the officers' mess, the atmosphere of danger on the horizon, the opportunity held out to prove one's courage in the adventure of combat in the air. Not that he had actually been engaged in action yet . . . but the time would come. This week he was home on leave; he'd come into Renchester today to take Pauline back to Briardale House for the weekend. They'd popped into Burridge's for a quick lunch.

"By the way," he said now, "Mother asked me to warn you that the house is more like a school nowadays. Personally, I'd call it a zoo. The kids start yelling about six in the morning."

There had been a good deal of comment, much of it slightly malicious, among the Mawtons' former Parklands neighbors, when a group of evacuees from the slum district was billeted at Briardale House last autumn. This event was generally felt to be a fitting consequence to Henry Mawton's ill-timed venture into the squirearchy. But the people who said (smiling behind their hands), "The poor Mawtons, fancy having all those children dumped on them"—or, "What a shame . . . Just when they'd got the place looking so lovely," underestimated Lily Mawton's capabilities.

And now, when Pauline remarked: "I hope they aren't ruining the house. I should think it would break your mother's heart to see grubby finger marks over everything," Clive replied:

"Oh, don't feel sorry for Mother! Those kids have given her a new lease of life. She always did like making umpteen pounds of jam, and bottling quantities of fruit, you know—well, now at last she's got her own private regiment to do justice to it all! And since the gardeners were called up, she's got the evacuees organized into mowing the lawns and clipping hedges. They love it, too. I think some of them had scarcely seen a blade of grass before they came to Briardale, poor little things. Most of them lived in those awful tenements behind the Infirmary."

"I don't believe I've ever been down there," said Pauline, pushing aside her rather unappetizing portion of fish. Meals in general were much less tempting since food rationing had been introduced.

"I used to drive that way every morning en route to the factory," Clive said. "By the way, I suppose you've heard that we're halving our output of fizzy drinks at the factory in order to use the rest of the space to make munitions?"

Pauline nodded. "There are lots of jokes going around about that—mostly on the lines of gunpowder getting into the lemonade."

Clive sat back in his chair as the waitress brought their pudding: lemon sponge with lumpy custard—made with dried milk, Pauline guessed.

"Father's really throwing himself into the war effort, now he's finally convinced of Hitler's dishonorable intentions," Clive went on. "He's even joined the Briardale Home Guard, and rushes about the village in khaki on the weekends, brandishing a .303 rifle, and helping to build tank traps on the roads." Suddenly, Clive thought of something his father had told him that morning. "You remember the very first time we met?" he asked Pauline.

She answered in a dramatic voice. "How could I ever forget it? I remember telling you to send round the bill for the broken gatepost. And what an absolute idiot I felt when I tried to start the car again and it was still in reverse gear!"

She laughed, and Clive smiled reminiscently. Pauline warmed towards him. Be careful, she told herself. Just because two people smile over an experience they happen to have shared together, that doesn't mean they're falling in love. . . .

"Actually, I wasn't thinking so much of the contretemps with the gatepost," he said. "Remember that German we picked up at the station—who'd come to study our factory methods?"

Pauline wrinkled her brow. "Um—yes. Vaguely."

"Hoffman, he was called: Erich Hoffman. Well, Father had a visit about him last week from a chap in our Intelligence Service. Apparently Hoffman was a spy; they have a dossier on his activities. He made a practice of touring British factories ostensibly to study engineering methods. They almost caught up on him—this chap told Father he was over here when war broke out, but he managed to escape back to Germany through Southern Ireland."

"A spy!" Pauline exclaimed. "But—he was so ordinary. Such an inoffensive boy. I can't believe he was a spy. Anyway, what on earth would he be spying on in Renchester?"

Clive shrugged. "The shipyards, I suppose."

Pauline poured out coffee, then looked at Clive over the rim of her cup. She decided this was the moment to break her news.

"Uniform suits you, Clive," she began.

Clive looked suspicious. "Flattery?"

She fiddled with her coffee spoon. "I was just wondering whether I'll look as handsome in mine."

"*Yours?* Your uniform?"

"Mmm. I've joined up. I'm going into the WRNS. The Senior Service—to you."

Pauline had expected Clive to be surprised, but he seemed positively startled.

"What on earth made you decide to do that?"

She felt a spurt of resentment at his tone. "The same sort of motives that made you volunteer for the air force, I suppose," she retorted crisply. Then she looked at him shrewdly. "A mixture of motives—isn't that right? Patriotism, wanting to help win the war—all that, of course. But less admirable reasons, too. I can't absolutely pose as a sort of Grace Darling or Florence Nightingale. You know I've felt for some time that my life was rather pointless and empty—well, here's a chance to change it. Then again, I want to join the WRNS rather than any of the other women's services, the ATS or the WAAF for instance, and if I waited until I was called up, I wouldn't be given the option of choosing between them.

At least I'm being perfectly honest about it. Perhaps one virtue cancels out the lack of another?"

"This is quite a surprise." Clive signaled the waitress for his bill, and brought his billfold out of a pocket of his jacket, where the silver pilot's wings were sewn. "I suppose this means I shan't be able to count on seeing you in future when I'm home . . . unless our leaves coincide."

Why, Pauline thought, he sounds almost peevish. Could it be that he liked the thought of a girl friend patiently waiting at home for him each time he came on leave? A girl friend in uniform wouldn't be quite the same thing. . . . She smiled to herself as Clive helped her into her coat, and they went out through the swing door of the restaurant.

Clive's car was standing around the corner from Burridge's. He had sold his Lagonda when he joined up, and now had a dark green MG. Petrol was rationed these days; he'd saved up a few precious gallons for this leave. They didn't talk as they got into the car and drove off.

Clive *was* feeling rather peevish—"browned off," as they said in the mess. It was sickening to think he wouldn't be able to count on Pauline's being at home in future. And what had she meant when she said his motives in joining up were "the same sort" as hers? Clive had built up a very satisfactory self-portrait of a dashing young pilot officer; he didn't like Pauline's suggestion that it wasn't pure patriotism that had made him join the air force. For, of course, he knew too well that was true. Nowadays, he often wondered how he'd ever stuck the humdrum routine of his job at the factory. Compared with the interest and excitement of flying, it seemed, in retrospect, deadly dull. Sometimes—though Clive and his fellow pilots didn't think about the future all that often—he wondered how he'd ever fit into ordinary civilian life again. From Hurricanes to fizzy lemonade would be quite a crash landing. . . .

The silence in the car was becoming noticeable, creating an atmosphere, and Clive made a conventional remark in order to break it.

They were speeding along the bypass now.

"One thing about petrol rationing, it's cleared away the traffic jams. I remember this road on bank holidays. Couldn't move an inch!"

Pauline agreed with him readily, and they succeeded in dispelling the uncomfortable feeling. After all, it was silly to sulk or quarrel during Clive's brief leave. She determined to be as pleasant as possible for the rest of the weekend.

The sports car raced along the country roads. There were yellow-pollened catkins in the hedges. Horse-chestnut trees had put out their sticky buds. Everything looked green and fresh—and peaceful. And yet, if one looked more closely, there were the signs of war in this quiet countryside. Near Briardale village there was a meadow occupied by Frisian cows and their straggle-legged calves, large enough for enemy aircraft to land in. Concrete blocks had been placed at intervals among the lush grass as part of the anti-invasion precautions. Signposts, too, at every crossroads stood pointing blindly to the four points of the compass. Briardale Village Stores had the word *Briardale* removed from its frontage. An enemy parachutist would not be helped on his way.

Was it possible, Pauline wondered, observing these things, that England could be invaded? That the blue sky could fill with white parachutes as thick as fleecy clouds? That jack-booted German storm troopers should march through the narrow lanes and drink their beer outside the Dog and Fox? Would the church bells ever ring to herald the threatened invasion? Would the home guard ever find their weekend maneuvers turned into the reality of guerrilla tactics in the hills and valleys, and hand-to-hand fighting in the streets? Such things had happened in Norway . . . Holland . . . Belgium . . . and today they were happening in France. That song people had shouted a little while ago, what was it?—"We're going to hang out the washing on the Siegfried Line"— seemed a very empty boast now. It wasn't Germany's Siegfried Line that had broken, it was France's Maginot Line, her defense against Nazi attack along her eastern frontier.

And yet—here in England the war seemed strangely distant still. No wonder everyone had talked of "the phoney war." There was no sign as yet of Hitler's threatened *Luftwaffe* attack on Britain. The Russian invasion of Finland last November, and the Finns' fierce and unexpectedly successful defense of their homeland, had taken place in a remote, snowbound landscape. The dramatic hunting of the *Graf Spee,* the great German battleship which had finally been scuttled at the mouth of the River Plate, happened two continents away. Britain still waited and watched for the war to cross her threshold.

Pauline shivered.

"Cold?" Clive asked. "Nearly home now. There'll be

a log-fire in the drawing room. We're using up dead apple boughs from the orchard."

They swept up the drive of Briardale House. Clive sounded his horn, a warning to stray evacuees. Lily Mawton appeared at the open door to welcome them. Clive reached into the back of the car for Pauline's suitcase, and kissed her quickly on the cheek. It was a gesture to show that there were no hard feelings.

What Price Glory?

The news from France could not have been worse. The Germans had occupied Paris four days ago. Marshal Pétain had surrendered to Hitler.

On June 18, 1940, Winston Churchill made a memorable broadcast. Throughout Britain, people switched on their radios to listen to the Prime Minister's inspiring message. He spoke solemnly of ". . . the colossal military disaster which occurred when the French High Command failed to withdraw the Northern Armies from Belgium at the moment when they knew the French front was decisively broken at Sedan and on the Meuse. This delay entailed the loss of fifteen or sixteen French divisions and threw out of action for the critical period the whole of the British Expeditionary Force . . ."

Then he spoke of that great deliverance which still seemed as though it were a miracle: "Our Army and one hundred and twenty thousand French troops were rescued by the Royal Navy from Dunkirk . . ."

Dunkirk! During the last days of May and the first days of June, Dunkirk had become a name familiar in every household . . . familiar as Agincourt. Dunkirk: the miracle of the little ships, when volunteers from every part of Britain—weekend yachtsmen, retired sailors, fishermen, captains and crews of pleasure steamers—carried over 335,000 men to safety, away from the beaches of death where they had been driven in defeat.

The Gray family was gathered around the wireless in the living room at Povey Street. They had just finished supper—"rissoles again!" Thomas Gray had grumbled as he screwed off the top of the ketchup bottle. Now, as the Prime Minister pronounced the name of Dunkirk, Eva offered up a silent prayer of gratitude. Ken, her Ken, Lance-Corporal Martin, dispatch rider in the armored corps, had been among those 335,000 men snatched from death, while the enemy planes screamed overhead. He was safe . . . for the time being.

". . . the battle in France has been lost."

At the other side of Renchester, in St. Oswald's Terrace, Suzanne Sinclair and her father were listening to the broadcast too. Suzanne had a few days' leave from her job in London. Her father found it curiously difficult to discover anything definite about this work: Suzanne never volunteered any information, and answered his questions about it vaguely. At this moment, Suzanne's thoughts were with Aunt Clothilde and Cousin Raoul, and their beloved city, where the Germans now marched in

triumph down the boulevards. She heard again her aunt's
voice: "Five times in a hundred years . . ." And now the
German guns had sounded once more over Notre Dame,
over the Arc de Triomphe, across the Seine, over the
rooftops of the Rue de Fleurus. . . .

Listening to Churchill's words, hearing again the voice
of Aunt Clothilde, Suzanne was proud to think that soon
she would be helping her mother's countrymen in their
terrible misfortune. She was glad she had volunteered
and been chosen to do the work she could not talk about,
even to her father.

In her pleasant house at Parklands, Nancy Harriman
had retired to bed early. She switched on her portable
radio in its blue leather case, and put aside the book she
had been trying to read—succeeding only in following the
same sentence over and over again.

"Our Army and one hundred and twenty thousand
French troops were rescued by the Royal Navy from
Dunkirk . . ."

But not Stanley Harriman. Stan was one of the unlucky
ones. He had been among the four thousand British and
French soldiers who stayed in Calais to hold the town as
long as possible, and protect the rear of the escaping
army. Calais was defended to the last. The British briga-
dier in command was given one hour to surrender. He
spurned the offer. There were four days of desperate fighting, with hand-to-hand combat in the streets. At last,
silence fell upon the ravaged town; the resistance was at
an end. Only thirty unwounded survivors were rescued
by the navy. Stanley Harriman was not one of them. Nor

was he among those who were taken prisoner by the Germans. He was shot down by a sniper's bullet in a narrow street of that seaside town, which very recently had been known to him merely as the terminus of one of the Channel ferries.

Nancy Harriman knew now the sorrow Julia Cortley had experienced, the sorrow Lily Mawton feared, the sorrow that hovered over so many homes.

The voice of the Prime Minister continued: ". . . the Battle of France is over. I expect that the Battle of Britain is about to begin. . . . The whole fury and might of the enemy must very soon be turned on us . . ."

Clive Mawton stood in the saloon bar of The White Hart, a glass of mild and bitter in his hand. This pub, somewhere in the south, was where he and his comrades gathered in their off-duty time to swap experiences, tell tall stories punctuated with RAF slang, drink, play darts, trade secondhand cars.

Here was Sam—

> *Sam balancing his beer*
> *Upon his chin:*
> *Sam somersaulting past the chandelier*
> *Performing his flat spin.*

Here, too, was Johnny—

> *Fetch out no shroud*
> *For Johnny-in-the-cloud;*
> *And keep your tears*
> *For him in after years.*

—laughing at the climax of a joke, gesturing to demonstrate some aerial antic.

Through a radio on the bar counter, normally switched on only for the racing results, Churchill spoke now of these young airmen.

". . . I look forward confidently to the exploits of our fighter pilots—these splendid men, this brilliant youth— who will have the glory of saving their native land, their island home, and all they love, from the most deadly of attacks."

The indomitable voice continued:

". . . Hitler knows that he will have to break us in this island or lose the war. . . . Let us therefore brace ourselves to our duties, and so bear ourselves that, if the British Empire and its Commonwealth last for a thousand years, men will still say, 'This was their finest hour.' "

The broadcast was over.

Clive swilled around the beer at the bottom of his glass, then drained it dry. Someone—one of the Sams, one of the Johnnies—called for another round of drinks. Someone else made a joke—"What price glory, you splendid chaps?" The responsive laughter came quickly, gratefully, to cover up the emotion that had been aroused.

The news program followed, and afterwards Air Marshal Sir Philip Joubert spoke about the prospects of an air attack on Britain. To all those who listened, the threat of air raids and invasion seemed very close.

Meanwhile, in Germany, Field Marshal Goering, Commander of the *Luftwaffe,* boasted to Hitler that it would take only a few weeks to smash the RAF from the sky. The German planes were ready to launch their attack.

Along the coasts of France and Belgium, German troops and landing barges assembled, and crack parachute divisions were brought west, ready for the invasion of Britain which would take place as soon as the RAF was defeated.

Bonne Chance

Although Suzanne had been working in London for over six months, she had met Gordon only occasionally during that time. This was partly because they both worked long hours, and meetings were difficult to arrange. But mostly it was because Suzanne wanted—now more than ever—to avoid emotional entanglement. She felt she must remain free and single-minded. She wanted to dedicate herself to her new work. Whatever hopes Gordon had held that by seeing each other in London, away from the environment of Renchester, the situation between them might alter, these came to nothing.

One evening in that summer of 1940, feeling he must see her, he called unexpectedly at the house in Queen's Gate where Suzanne rented a bed-sitting-room. He found her in the middle of a grand clearout. A wastepaper tub overflowed with torn-up letters, old bank statements, receipts, duplicate photograph prints . . . the miscellania that accumulates around us day by day.

"Moving house?" Gordon wondered if she had found new digs.

Suzanne shook her head, pushing her dark hair back from her face and scrambling to her feet to greet him. "This suits me all right"—she waved one hand around the room, with its barely adequate furniture, worn carpet, and long windows that opened onto an ornamental balcony.

Gordon thought the room strangely impersonal. Apart from an adjustable reading lamp, crouched on the table like a huge black spider, and a reproduction of a Utrillo painting—the "Rue de Village"—Suzanne had left it as it was when she first moved in. This seemed out of character; Gordon knew that usually she took trouble to make her surroundings attractive. Under her influence, the old house in St. Oswald's Terrace had been a charming home. This room was scarcely comfortable; it looked almost conventual—or else as though she did not expect to remain in it very long. Yet her job, whatever it was (he'd never succeeded in finding out much about it) would presumably last the duration of the war. And God knows, that seems as though it's going to be long enough, he thought. Why, there wasn't even a photograph on view; nothing personal at all.

"Actually, I'm going away for a week or so." Suzanne offered cigarettes, and took one herself. "Part of our office is being moved to the outskirts of London in case the bombing starts. I'm helping with the move." She leaned forward to light her cigarette from Gordon's match, wondering if her words sounded sufficiently plausible. "It seemed a suitable moment to sort out my own stuff," she finished.

"I see." Gordon glanced at the wastepaper tub. "Well, all *that* should help the salvage drive."

Suzanne swept a collection of theater programs piled on the arm of her chair into the junk heap. "It's positively alarming, the way possessions mount up . . . even when you try your best to keep free of them."

Gordon looked at her curiously. She seemed to be speaking thoughts out loud rather than talking to him.

Then he announced: "I've come to take you out. Esmé Beaton—you know, the Beatons' glamorous daughter—is in London, working as a secretary with ENSA. She phoned me and asked me along this evening—I thought you might like to go too, and she said she'd love to see both of us."

"Esmé Beaton? I'd no idea she was in London. Yes, I'd like to come."

Yes, Gordon thought, you'd like to come, so long as we're not to be alone . . . so long as there are other people to insulate you from—getting involved. Still, he would rather see Suzanne in the company of other people than not at all. . . .

So they took a bus to Chelsea, and wandered down a narrow street off the King's Road, peering for the right address. The two-roomed flat was in the basement of a tall gray house. Suzanne followed Gordon down a flight of stone steps into an area decorated with dustbins and tired hydrangeas in yellow tubs.

"It's as good as living in an air-raid shelter," Esmé assured them as she opened the door. "I shall just sit tight when the bombs start falling!"

She was wearing black velvet trousers and an emerald-green jersey; she enjoyed dramatic clothes. She introduced the girl who shared her flat. Lorna Prescott was pretty, with sleek fair hair that hung to her shoulders in page-boy style. She worked in ENSA too. There was a boy friend of Lorna's there as well, an American studying at London University.

Suzanne thought the flat reflected the characters of its two occupants; both Esmé and Lorna were vivacious and gay. The walls were painted white; curtains, rugs, and cushions were brightly colored. Lorna was clever with her hands and had made lampshades that were perched on empty demijohn bottles. Someone had given Esmé two posters with wartime slogans. She had pinned one just inside the front door (*Walls Have Ears*) and the other in the bathroom (*Careless Talk Costs Lives*).

Suzanne glanced across at Gordon and they smiled at each other with their eyes; it was all far removed from Renchester. Suzanne wondered whether Esmé would ever go home again except for visits. She obviously loved life in London.

Most of the evening, the conversation was lighthearted and they laughed a good deal. Lorna played gramophone records: Vera Lynn singing "Yours"; inevitably, Richard Addinsell's "Warsaw Concerto," from *Dangerous Moonlight,* the film based on the Poles' resistance to the Germans; Bing Crosby crooning "South of the Border"—

> *That's where I fell in love*
> *When stars above*
> *Came out to play . . .*

"I adore drippy songs, don't you?" Lorna asked everyone.

The last note of "South of the Border" died away, and she went over to the pile of records again.

"What a bore it is having to change records and turn them over every other minute—like frying pancakes," she complained. "I wish someone would invent records that went on playing for ages." She squinted at a label. "Oh, this one is *marvelous*. The sort of tune that you get on the brain for days—"

It was Jean Sablon, singing "The Last Time I Saw Paris."

"Sob stuff!" Andy MacIntyre, the American, grinned at Lorna. "You're such a smart girl, Lorna—how can you fall for these corny ballads?"

Lorna threw a record at him. It hit a table leg and broke in pieces. Esmé examined the label anxiously.

" 'There'll Always Be an England'—oh, that's all right. It always made me wriggle, it's so embarrassingly patriotic."

Suzanne knew the songs were corny. All of them. Andy was right. But it was queer—in spite of this, they were sincere, too, those songs. And this particular one—"The Last Time I saw Paris"—meant more to her than any of the others.

Gordon happened to look at Suzanne as the record spun around, and was puzzled by the expression on her face.

A little while later, Andy made the first move. "I'm fire-watching tonight," he announced. "We take it in turns to sit on top of the college roof. They even rope in neutrals, you see!"

They all knew he must have volunteered for fire-watching duty, and liked him for it.

Then Gordon asked the direct question. "When is America coming into the war?"

Andy shrugged his shoulders and replied lightly: "Don't ask me. I missed the last boat home."

No one chose to follow up this line of conversation. Lorna, for one, was glad. She knew how Andy had grown to dread the argument. He was for Roosevelt, and Roosevelt was in favor of America's declaring war on Hitler. But America was a big country, and not every American by any means felt as President Roosevelt and Andy MacIntyre did. In November last year, the President had signed the American Neutrality Bill, but in words and in deeds that stopped short of actually infringing her neutrality, he had since demonstrated his country's sympathy for the Allies.

The party broke up, and Gordon saw Suzanne back to Kensington. She was rather silent; he thought she must be tired.

"Good night," he said as they parted. "Good night, Suzanne."

"*Au 'voir*," she whispered, and hoped it would be true.

She climbed the long flight of stairs to her room, where now everything was in order. She didn't want to leave untidy ends behind her for other people to clear up. "We cannot safeguard you in any way. You will be entirely on your own." The voice of the briefing officer had been cold and impersonal. Suzanne had nodded and answered, "Yes." Yes, she understood.

The last time I saw Paris . . . Lorna had said that tune got on your brain. It had certainly got on hers! When at last Suzanne slept that night, the record was still going round.

Esmé and Lorna were washing up glasses and cups and saucers in their minute kitchen.

"You're in love with Gordon What's-his-name, aren't you?" Lorna said suddenly, whisking the soap-saver around the washing-up bowl.

The saucer Esmé had been drying jumped out of her hands and crashed to the floor.

"How did you guess?"

Lorna got out the dustpan and brush. "Not very difficult," she replied, sweeping up the bits of broken china. "I know you pretty well by now. And I've never seen you look the way you did tonight when you were talking to him."

Esmé watched Lorna deposit the broken saucer in the garbage pail under the sink.

"It's no use," she said despairingly. "He adores Suzanne. He *likes* me, I know—but that's all. He probably thinks of me as a child still. He used to visit us at home when I was still a schoolgirl." She hung the wet drying-up cloth over the top of the gas cooker. "Did you see the way they smiled at each other when I was showing off our poster décor? As though—as though I was a little girl with a Wendy house!"

Lorna laughed. "Don't be melodramatic, m'dear. I must say, I don't exactly see what makes Gordon "adore" Suzanne. Personally, I thought she was rather dreary. Good-looking, of course. But she didn't have much to say, did she? What does she do?"

Lorna was apt to judge quiet people as dreary and noisy people as "fun."

Esmé shrugged. "I don't know exactly. Some job in the

War Office, I think. Nine till five in Whitehall, I suppose."

"Oh. Sounds deadly."

"No," Esmé said, almost in spite of herself, "Suzanne's really a terribly nice person, and she's got heaps of character." She grinned suddenly. "You mustn't try to comfort my unrequited love by running down the Other Woman!"

"Oh, well—if you can joke about it, it can't be all that bad," Lorna declared, emptying the washing-up water.

Esmé didn't reply. She watched the water swirl around the plug hole and gurgle away. It *was* that bad. She'd always thought Gordon was a wonderful person, ever since those days when he used to visit them at Parklands. She could still blush at the memory of some of the brash remarks she used to insert into the conversation round the dinner table in order to make him notice her.

"I'm glad I'm not in love with Andy," Lorna said thoughtfully. "It would be too much—effort. He's fun as a boy friend, we laugh a lot and have a gay time. Being in love would be too much like hard work!"

But as she said this, she wondered if she were being honest with herself. She had a suspicion that her feelings for Andy went deeper than she realized.

A few days later. Dusk on an airfield somewhere in England. A girl called "Marie Clavion" stood waiting to board the plane that would take her to Occupied France. Suzanne Sinclair had left her identity behind in the room where she had changed a short while ago. Everything she wore now—the cream-colored raincoat, silk head scarf, shoes, handbag—was French. She carried a false identification card, a supply of French money. Even her powder compact had come from a shop in the Rue de Rivoli. Nothing had been overlooked.

The plane taxied along the runway. This was it. There were two other agents waiting to board with her. Suzanne did not know who they were—simply two British agents, like herself, bound on a special mission to help the French Resistance. Each of them had his own job to carry out. None of them might return.

"Good luck! Happy landings!" a WAAF officer shouted after them as they went on board.

"*Bonne chance!*" a French voice called.

The plane was air-borne. A line of trees, deep-etched in the darkening sky, fell sharply away. They turned towards the coast of France.

Singing Lesson

Renchester had its first air raid in October, 1940. The first of many. Scarcely a night passed that autumn and winter without the siren's wail warning of enemy bombers approaching. The dockland area suffered most; German Intelligence had discovered that submarines were being built at Renchester. The steep rows of little houses huddled around the river mouth, dense as a crowd at a ship's launching in prewar days, were shattered and destroyed. Brick and mortar, slate and stone, fell apart, to reveal interior walls covered in patterned wallpaper; light brackets clinging to strips of plaster; pictures in gilded frames hanging crazily askew. Furniture was scattered into the streets as though from overturned dolls' houses: a wardrobe agape, still filled with clothes; an armchair with its antimacassar; a cot decorated with transfers of Mickey Mouse and Donald Duck. Flames licked greedily over the scenes of ruin. Each night the red glow in the sky above the docks could be seen as far away as the new housing estates.

The rest of the town got its share of high-explosive bombs and incendiaries. In the High Street, plate-glass windows were shattered and replaced by temporary coverings, with notices that read: *Business As Usual.* The north end of the station received a direct hit that demolished a row of goods-trains. Burridge's furniture depository was burned out. There were gaps like missing teeth among the houses in the Povey Street area. Up at Parklands, and on the new housing estates, they were luckier; only the stray raider came their way.

Now the wisdom of last year's evacuation of the downtown schoolchildren was proved; now the brick-and-concrete surface shelters that had been erected in the streets, the Anderson shelters in gardens and backyards, the huge trench-shelter in the Memorial Recreation Ground, came into their own. Now ARP drill became reality instead of mere exercise; working stirrup pumps, donning tin helmets, fire-watching, digging for victims trapped among the rubble: all this became routine. And the air-raid warning, the all-clear, and the anti-aircraft barrage of gunfire formed the continuous background music to the drama that was played out each night.

There had been talk of Renchester High School evacuating its pupils into the country, but the plan came to nothing. The school had turned its huge cellars into an air-raid shelter, and if the siren sounded during the day, the girls were immediately hustled below ground level. Here they sat on long benches, and the youngest were given barley sugar to suck. To them, "barley sugar" became synonymous with the first wail of the siren.

Each girl had to bring her gas mask to school every day, and gas-mask inspection became as regular as lost-property inspection. To see if your gas mask would function properly, in case the dreaded poison gas was ever used by the enemy, you put it over your face, held a piece of paper to the end of the snout, and breathed in. If the paper adhered to the snout, all was well.

There were other signs of the times in school. Instead of swapping cigarette cards ("Kings and Queens of England," "Wild Flowers," and send threepence for your cigarette-card album), you exchanged jagged pieces of shrapnel that had fallen during the night, relics of the anti-aircraft shellfire. Janet Murdoch was much envied among the members of the Lower Fourth because she possessed a German helmet which her brother had brought home during one of his leaves. Instead of collecting car numbers, you learned to recognize airplanes by their shape: Wellington, Spitfire, Hurricane . . . Heinkel, Messerschmidt, Dornier. . . . And a good many of the rules about school uniform were relaxed in the interests of the Government campaign to "Make Do and Mend."

Some things stayed the same, however. Singing lessons, for instance. Bombs might fall, but the High School girls still sang their way through the regulation repertoire, beginning with "Cherry Ripe" and ending with "Linden Lea."

Singing lessons for the Lower Fourth took place on Wednesday mornings. And on one particular Wednesday morning early in December, the sprightly strains of "Nymphs and Shepherds" could be heard echoing from the hall. Here, Flora Stanford, Janet Murdoch, and Anna Jelinck were standing together in the back row of chairs ranged round the piano. Miss Greaves, the music mistress, was pounding out the tune:

Nymphs and she-ep-erds, co-ome away,
Come away, come away,
Nymphs and she-ep-erds . . .

Flora grimaced at Janet in mid-song, to indicate her disapproval. It wasn't her idea of a decent tune. Why couldn't they have something sensible, like "Heart of Oak" or "Men of Harlech"? Nymphs and shepherds, indeed!

Janet raised her eyebrows and rolled her eyes upwards in eloquent reply to Flora's grimace. Then, quite suddenly, a wild fit of giggles overcame both of them as they launched into the next part of the song:

For this, this is Flor-ora's holiday,
This is Flor-or-a's holiday.
This is Flor-or-a's ho-o-ol-i-day!

Even Anna, who had been singing the strange English words carefully in her usual serious manner, looked up and caught the infectious hilarity. The three girls stood with shaking shoulders and scarlet faces, songsheets rattling as they tried to hide their giggles behind them. Singing, of course, was quite impossible; as a result there was a noticeable decrease in volume from the back row. At length the inevitable happened. Janet's suppressed laughter burst out in a loud snort, followed by explosions from Flora and Anna.

Everyone turned to stare; Miss Greaves lifted her hands from the piano, and the singing died away uneasily.

"May we share the joke?" The music mistress's voice was icy.

Janet struggled to speak. "It—it's the words, Miss

Greaves, the words!" she gasped wildly. "F-Flora . . .
F-Flora's h-holiday!"

Miss Greaves frowned in exasperation. "Really, Janet,
how can you be so childish? Control yourself. You'd
better come into the front row."

Still heaving with submerged giggles, Janet came into
the front row. Miss Greaves turned back to the keyboard.
"We'll go back to the beginning," she announced.

But now that the whole form had seen the joke, the
situation was hopeless. Everyone burst into a great roar
of laughter as soon as they reached the fatal lines.

Miss Greaves stopped playing. She had spent last night
fire-watching on the school roof; she was tired, and her
head ached.

"Very well," she said at last. "We'll abandon 'Nymphs
and Shepherds' for this week and go on to 'The Ballad
of London River.' I don't think you'll find any feeble
jokes to giggle over in that."

The word *feeble* had an immediate sobering effect, for
in current High School language it happened to be the
most insulting adjective you could use. Miss Greaves,
who knew this perfectly well, sighed with relief as the
class began the first verse of the new song:

> *From the Cotswolds, from the Chilterns,*
> *From your valleys and your springs,*
> *Flow down, O London River,*
> *To the seagull's silver wings . . .*

Even Flora considered the tune a pretty good one. They
were practicing the song for the Commemoration Day
concert at the end of term, in a fortnight's time. Commemoration Day was held in honor of the school's first

headmistress, a late Victorian lady called Miss Keats. Her portrait looked down upon the singing class from the far end of the hall. Miss Keats had been very fond of anemones, and it was a school tradition that on Commemoration Day, each form-room should be decorated with bowls of anemones. In the evening, the flowers used to be sent to Renchester Infirmary for the children's ward. Of course, it was difficult to get anemones in December. Renchester's leading florist used to order a special consignment from France. This year, for the first time since Miss Keats' death, there would be no bowls of anemones in the form-rooms.

Parents and old girls of the school came to the concert on Commem. Day. Some of the old girls were really old, so that you could hardly imagine them as schoolgirls, in gym tunics and wrinkled stockings. But others had left school only a term or so ago; *they* often looked as though they were dressing up as old girls.

Pauline would be home on a few days' leave just before Christmas; in a letter to Flora she'd promised to come along to the concert. Flora hoped she might come in her WRNS uniform. But Pauline was always glad to get into "civvies" when she was at home; she said it was one of the best things about being on leave.

The rest of that December day at the High School passed without any special excitement. There was no air raid. Flora had had a sneaking hope that the siren might sound during Latin, for she hadn't learned the new declension.

At the end of the afternoon, Janet and Anna set off together, as usual, their satchels filled with books for revision prep. End-of-term exams began the following week. Anna got off the bus first as she always did. Janet's cheerful call, "See you tomorrow!" rang in her ears as she turned into Derwent Crescent.

She clicked open the garden gate and went round to the kitchen door. Her father and mother were in the kitchen. Her father was standing in the middle of the room, talking excitedly while her mother placidly stirred a large pan of vegetable soup.

"I reach the house—Miss Maloney, 47 The Avenue—I know it well, I can see it here"—Josef tapped his forehead—"always with lace curtains at the windows and with an electric bell which does not ring."

"So—you reach the house. And then?" Her mother turned to greet Anna with a smile.

"So the house—it is not there! It is gone. No lace curtains, no electric bell . . . nothing. There is only such a pile of rubble, and on the gatepost still remains the brass plate with Miss Maloney's name on it, so shiny, like it was polished every day."

Antonia Jelinck shook her head as she tasted a spoonful of the soup. "This war! So much trouble. Such waste."

"Is that why you're home early, Father?" asked Anna, shrugging her school satchel from her shoulders.

"Yes, my child. There are two pianos there I was to look at. The Blüthner, that was for the advanced pupils; the upright was for the little childrens . . ." He sat down on a chair and stared into space.

Supper was a more silent meal than usual. Afterwards, Anna cleared a space for herself at the table, got out her geography books, and revised Australia.

The air-raid warning sounded soon after the nine o'clock news. Antonia Jelinck raised her eyes to the ceiling. "So—they have not forgotten us tonight." Before long, they heard the heavy throb of planes and the *crump-crump* of the anti-aircraft guns. The raid lasted about an hour. Just before the all-clear sounded, they heard a lone bomber overhead, limping through the sky with an uneven drone.

"He is crippled, that one," Anna's father remarked.

Then it happened. There was the long, unearthly shriek of bombs falling slantwise across the rooftops. The German bomber, hit by gunfire and caught in a maze of searchlights, jettisoned its last stick of bombs . . . into the heart of the new housing estates.

Josef pushed Antonia and Anna to the ground, and the three of them crawled under the stout kitchen table. Huge explosions sounded all round them. There was a crash and tinkling of broken glass as a blast shattered the kitchen window. A few moments, and it was all over. Gradually the gunfire ceased. And at last they heard the all-clear.

The Jelincks were lucky. The bombs had passed over Derwent Crescent. They'd missed Laburnum Close, too. At number eight Laburnum Close, the family crawled thankfully out of the Anderson shelter—mother, father, a little girl with Shirley Temple curls, and Mary, the maid. This was Mary's last week in Renchester. She had been called up, and was going into the Land Army. . . . Back to the country at last, to the way of life she understood. Funny, that war could sometimes bring happiness as well as grief. . . .

But two bombs fell in Oakdene Gardens. One was a direct hit on the Murdochs' house. The ARP rescue squad worked until the early hours of the morning, when they at last discovered the bodies among the rubble. There were no survivors. As they dug, they came upon the torn-off binding of an atlas. Janet had been revising for the geography exam, too. The atlas was marked inside the front cover—

> *Janet Clare Murdoch*
> *19 Oakdene Gardens, Sandilands Estate,*
> *Renchester. Northshire. England. Great Britain.*
> *Europe. The World. The Universe. Space.*

The shape of Australia, the principal rivers of America, the changing boundaries of political maps—Janet had passed beyond all these things.

A Pair of Shoes

Simmons' Shoe Shop was next door to Marks & Spencer's. Pauline had seen the shoes she wanted in the shop window: black low-heeled oxfords which she would have scorned to wear a little while ago. But they were just the thing with WRNS uniform. *For Service Wear,* announced the showcard beside them. Pauline was wearing mufti this afternoon. It felt wonderful to be out of navy blue for a while. Especially not to be wearing her blue gabardine cap. She never had liked wearing hats. The thick cotton Issue Hose, dubbed "plush" by the recruits, were a bit too much of a good thing, too: Pauline had decided to invest in some black silk stockings as well as a new pair of shoes.

This was the last day of her leave. She'd enjoyed it. She'd spent most of the time with her family, seen a few girl friends, and gone out with Tony Welsh one evening. Then there had been Commem. Day at the High School. How strange that had seemed without the anemones.

Pauline recalled how their vivid, stained-glass colors used to glow in every room. The headmistress, in her address after the commemoration prayers, had spoken of their absence as symbolic of wartime change—and challenge. She had reminded her listeners that anemones were supposedly the "lilies of the field" of which St. Matthew spoke, and quoted the passage from the New Testament which closed with words significant for the times: "Sufficient unto the day is the evil thereof."

There was one other customer in the shoe department, a girl trying on snowboots, the new craze this year for chilly feet, especially welcome to women going out on early factory shifts. Pauline was surprised when the girl spoke to her.

"Hello, Miss Stanford."

She couldn't think who the girl was—and yet her face did seem vaguely familiar. "Hallo," she replied briefly, and walked across the shop to look at a display of slippers: *The Ideal Christmas Gift,* said the placard hung above them.

Marion Gray—for it was she—bent her head to examine the snowboots the assistant had brought for her inspection, and to hide the color that rushed to her cheeks. Pauline Stanford didn't seem to think she was worth talking to! Even though they only knew each other by sight, they could have exchanged a sentence or two. . . .

"I'll have the ones with the sealskin trimming," Marion told the assistant. "And I'll pay by check."

The sealskin boots were more expensive than the others; still, she could afford them. She enjoyed being able to say, "I'll pay by check," too; she'd opened a bank account very recently. As she took her checkbook out of her handbag, she suddenly remembered a remark Eva had made that morning: *"You think you're so grand, don't you, with your precious checkbook and all . . ."*

They'd quarreled, she and Eva, at the breakfast table. It began when Eva announced that she was leaving Madame Rita's and going to work in the munitions factory.

Marion had stared at her sister in amazement. "But— you don't *have* to go into munitions!" she'd exclaimed. "You're exempt from call-up: you're a married woman . . ."

"What's that got to do with it?" Eva had retorted. "Just because I'm married doesn't make it any better—the fact that I spend all day pinning up women's hair when I could be doing something really useful."

"Oh, my!" Marion had pulled a face to show what she thought of this.

"And I don't care if it does sound priggish, either." Eva looked at her sister angrily. "I don't care what *you* think."

Here Mrs. Gray had interposed. "It's very right and proper, Evie love, that you want to do your bit for the war effort. We're proud of you . . . aren't we, Dad?"

Her husband had been busy looking through a seedsman's catalogue that the postwoman had brought that morning. He'd answered his wife's appeal with a vague nod. Recently, Thomas Gray had undergone a change for the better. It was the "Dig for Victory" campaign launched by the Government that had done it. Nowadays, he tended a quarter of an acre of English soil on one of the new allotments—strips of soil divided among town-dwellers throughout Britain: an echo, perhaps, of Domesday time. He dug and hoed, planted and weeded, and proudly brought home produce for the table. Prejudiced politics no longer dominated his thoughts. Instead, he debated the properties of different brands of fertilizer or weed-killer, and watched the weather anxiously in times of drought or frost.

"It didn't seem right—Ken away fighting, and me doing nothing to help," Eva had continued as her father returned to the paragraph describing a new variety of purple sprouting broccoli.

"Well, I think you're daft," Marion had declared. "Giving up a perfectly good job at Madame Rita's to go and make shells! Imagine getting out of bed on a cold morning for the early shift—brrh!"

Then Eva—mild, easy-going Eva—had suddenly spoken out. "Yes, you would think that," she told her sister hotly. "That's just the sort of selfish attitude I'd expect you to have, Marion Gray. You never think of anyone except yourself. Oh, we all know you're doing ever so well, thank you, sitting on your behind in Stanford's office in your nice, safe, cushy job. You think you're so grand, don't you, with your la-di-da voice, and your precious checkbook and all—the Post Office Savings Bank isn't good enough for *you*!"

"Evie!" her mother had protested. "There's no call to go on at Marion like that—"

Eva had shrugged. "Well, all I can say is that if I were her, I'd join one of the services—the ATS or the WAAF. . . . She might get to know a few boy friends then!"

This had stung Marion to the quick.

"Is that so? Well, you're not me—and I'm not you, thank goodness. *I* wouldn't marry a back-street garage hand . . ."

At this point, their father had frowned at the raised voices and angry words. "I can't stand all this row at breakfast time. It'll give me indigestion for the rest of the day. We get enough noise with Warbling Willy going off every night. Shut up, the pair of you."

They had shut up . . . but in the minds of the two sisters the quarrel continued.

It had upset Marion. She'd found it difficult to concentrate on her work that morning. Now, sitting in the shoe shop, waiting while her snowboots were parceled up, she experienced again something of the hot resentment she'd felt at Eva's thrust about her lack of boy friends.

Meanwhile, another assistant was serving Pauline Stanford.

"I'll take these," Pauline was saying, indicating a pair of black oxfords. "Put them on my account, will you? And I'd like them sent to my billet at Portsmouth."

The assistant waited to take down the address. "What rank, Madam?" she asked.

Pauline looked surprised. "Oh, don't bother about that. Just address them to Miss Stanford . . ."

"I'm sorry, Madam, but we have to put the rank of officer when sending service shoes. It's a shop rule——"

"Oh, very well. Put 'Wren Stanford,' then."

"Oh." The assistant, a middle-aged woman in a rusty black dress, looked embarrassed. "I'm afraid, in that case, Madam, we cannot sell you these particular shoes."

"Why ever not?"

"They're officers' shoes, Madam. We have other styles . . ."

"*Officers' shoes?*" Pauline's annoyed voice rang across the room. "I've never heard of anything so silly. Of course, I shall have these shoes if I want them."

Marion, in the act of departing, lingered to hear how the incident would end. She felt a certain glee. This was an unusual situation for Pauline Stanford to find herself in!

At Pauline's insistence, the assistant fetched the manager of the shop. The Stanfords were good customers; he was most apologetic—it was a rule devised by the manufacturer of the shoe; Simmons' was allowed to supply that style of black oxford to WRNS officers only. He was very sorry; there were other, similar styles in stock . . ."

But Pauline had heard enough. She was bored with the tiresome business. "I shall buy the shoes I want elsewhere," she said finally, and made a dignified exit.

As she passed Marion on her way out, she suddenly remembered who she was—the girl who worked in her father's office. She smiled at Marion, remembering that she'd last seen her in that wedding party at Burridge's, when she was lunching with Clive one day.

Then her thoughts switched to Clive. They had drifted apart lately. Pauline supposed it was inevitable. Their friendship had flourished so long as they saw each other a lot, went out together to parties—dances—film shows. But it had been a fair-weather friendship, after all, not deep enough to withstand a parting. It was certainly a case of "Out of sight, out of mind"—*not* "Absence makes the heart grow fonder." They still wrote to each other, but Pauline had noticed that Clive's letters were much cooler in tone recently. He'd mentioned another girl friend—Valerie, she was called. Oh, well, Pauline didn't intend to shed tears over that. They'd had some good times together, she and Clive; it was a relief to be able to drift apart without any painful scenes.

Pauline herself had made one or two new boy friends since she became a Wren. She'd met them at dances—naval officers on training courses, mostly. There was no one special, though. She'd made new girl friends, too, some of them very different from the sort of girls she'd known at school, and in the Parklands circle. The way you mixed with all sorts of people, so that you seemed to look at life from a wider point of view, was what Pauline liked most about being in the WRNS. The girls in her intake had been a very mixed bunch: ex-debs, shopgirls, office girls, women in their late twenties who seemed to her terribly self-assured and sophisticated; and girls who, like herself, had only recently left school. She'd found the communal life—the large dormitory, the noisy recreation room—rather overwhelming at first. She remembered with amusement her shocked surprise when she'd noticed that some of the girls slept in their under-clothes, instead of pajamas or nightdresses. Some of the language they used was pretty startling at times, too.

But, on the whole, she preferred the down-to-earth types to the ex-debs. The latter were inclined to huddle together in exclusive groups. But the down-to-earthers were always friendly and helpful. There was Marlene, for instance, the Cockney girl who had noticed her struggling with her stiff collar her very first morning in uniform, and had shown her how to cope with fastening the back stud—"Yer put yer stud through both 'oles first, ducks—shirt and collar. Nah put yer tie inside yer collar, an' join yer collar to yer stud . . ."

Pauline's work consisted of operating a teleprinter. In official jargon, she was a T/P op, responsible for sending out naval signals. After learning how to operate the teleprinter, she had been posted to the office of the C-in-C, Portsmouth. Here, in the closely guarded subterranean Fort Southwick, she worked in a large room alongside scores of other T/P ops. Much of the work was routine, often dull. Most of the messages were in code, and incomprehensible, in any case. But the times when their work suddenly became exciting and vital more than made up for the periods of dullness. The job demanded a good deal of skill; Pauline found she had especially to keep her wits about her when she was printing cipher groups on her chattering machine.

Outside Simmons' she paused, then decided to go along to the K Shoe Shop, at the end of the High Street. She passed by a greengrocer's, where the inevitable queue stretched into the street. Christmas trees were on sale, standing against the front of the shop like folded green umbrellas. But there would be no tangerines in silver paper this year, and no dates for dessert, after the plum pudding. There was fighting now where the date palms grew. A few days ago, the British Middle Eastern army, under General Wavell, had launched its attack on the Italian army in the Western Desert. Their aim was to prevent Italy from invading Egypt. Mussolini's troops had already invaded Greece.

A Merry Xmas! proclaimed a holly-decorated streamer

in Marks & Spencer's windows. That slogan—"Nothing Over Five Shillings"—no longer rang true. Woolworth's was no longer "the threepenny and sixpenny store," either. There were no more cheap goods imported from Japan now. In September, the Japanese had joined the Axis. This was a great blow; many people had believed Japan would join the Allies as she did during the 1914 war. Other shops, many with their windows newly patched-up, repeated the Christmas greeting. There were displays of gifts, decorations of tinsel ropes, cotton-wool snowflakes, shining glass balls. It would be the first time Pauline had spent Christmas away from home.

She reached the shoe shop and went inside.

"Can I help you?"

"I'd like some low-heeled black walking shoes to wear with WRNS uniform." Pauline paused, then added: "Incidentally, I am not a ranking officer. . . ."

A View of the Eiffel Tower

There were anemones on the flower seller's barrow at the corner of the Rue de Rivoli and the Rue du Louvre. Suzanne, returning despondently from another unrewarding visit to Montmartre, stopped, arrested by their glowing velvet petals. There was a cloud of fluffy yellow mimosa, too, redolent of the south and sunshine and careless luxury: mimosa, a paradox in wintry, occupied Paris. A German officer, warmly wrapped in his gray field coat, was buying an armful of the flowers for the girl hanging on his arm. She saw Suzanne looking at them, and lifted her chin with a brazen gesture that seemed to say: "Yes, I'm a *collaborateur*. So what?"

When they had gone, Suzanne approached the flower seller. *"Combien, madame, les anémones?"*

The old woman looked out shrewdly from the folds of her black shawl. "For you, *m'selle,* they are a gift."

"A gift!" Suzanne stared as a large bunch of anemones was put into her hand.

The old woman laid one forefinger along her nose. "A gift from *m'sieur*"—she indicated the retreating German officer. "I overcharged him four times for the mimosa, that one!"

Suzanne took the flowers and went on her way through the maze of little streets around St. Germain des Près. The flower seller was another one like her compatriot of the Paris Métro, who sat on a bench all day just inside the entrance to one of the underground stations, tripping German soldiers with her stick as they walked by. She averaged thirty trips a day, or so Marcel, the pastry cook, had told Suzanne.

Marcel's shop was Suzanne's base in Paris; she had a camp bed in an attic room that could be sealed off from the rest of the house, where Marcel lived with his wife and two small children. Not so long ago the window of Marcel's shop used to be filled with trays of mouth-watering gâteaux, brioches, éclairs, rhum babas, and sugared confectionery of every kind. His birthday cakes, decorated with inspiration, were ordered for every important anniversary party in the neighborhood. All that had gone now, melted into the nostalgic memory of things as they used to be—before the war, before the occupation. Now Marcel sold rye bread, and sometimes, when he could get the ingredients, a few plain cakes.

Suzanne had wanted the anemones for a purpose— they were the flowers Aunt Clothilde loved best. She walked right past Marcel's shop, as far as the Luxembourg Gardens and the Rue de Fleurus. Was she being imprudent, careless, in carrying out this little personal plan? She didn't think so. It seemed harmless enough.

It had snowed recently; the trees in the Luxembourg

Gardens, where in summer nursemaids sat minding their charges, were dripping with the thaw that had set in. Slush on the pavements made it treacherous underfoot.

Anemones! Commemoration Day at the High School! As she walked along, Suzanne had a vivid recollection of the school staff-room. She saw the creaking basket chairs with their flowered chintz cushions, the tray of coffee cups on the table. . . . There, if she had so decided, she might be sitting at this moment, writing out end-of-term reports: "Mary has worked well"; "Shirley must make a real effort to learn her verbs"; "Joyce's written work shows improvement, but her accent is poor" . . .

But this flashback to another world lasted only an instant. Suzanne was worried as she walked on through the narrow streets, patrolled by German police. Her contact, the agent to whom she was to pass her message, should have got in touch with her five days ago. Each day she went to Montmartre to look for the sign she was expecting. But the street artist in the little arcade off the Rue Gabrielle never displayed the picture she wanted to see. The Eiffel Tower was never there among the gaudy canvases showing sunsets, seascapes, emerald-green forests. Something must have gone wrong. All she could do was to wait and watch.

The rendezvous arranged for her return to Britain had gone by. She was time-expired. Now she would have to find her way home according to the instructions she had been given in case this happened. Her route would lie across the Pyrenees, into neutral Spain—then back to England. She had decided to wait in Paris another week before starting out on the first leg of this escape route, before leaving her attic room at Marcel's and going to the next address, in the suburb of Neuilly. She must not leave until she had given her unknown colleagues in the Resistance every chance of contacting her. The information she had been sent to pass on to them—that next month, a new target area was to be used for parachuting into France the arms they needed so badly—was vital.

She passed by a café that used to be a favorite haunt of students at the Sorbonne. She remembered it well. Now it was shuttered and deserted: the striped awnings, the round-topped tables with ashtrays advertising Cinzano, the eager, chattering, gesticulating crowd that used to flock there—all were gone. Suzanne sighed, because they were gone and because she was worried for the patriotic Frenchman in whose home she was lodging. She knew Marcel was becoming uneasy at her protracted stay. It was dangerous for him and for his family to have her staying in the house.

She reached the Rue de Fleurus, and stopped opposite the tall apartment building where her aunt lived. There was no one about, no sign of the concierge, who might have recognized her. She went through the arched doorway in the wall, across the cobbled courtyard, up the stairs to the third landing. A reproduction Louis XV armchair, over-decorated with gilded seashells clumsily carved, stood outside her aunt's front door.

Whenever she saw that chair, Suzanne remembered an incident that happened years ago, when she was a little girl. She had clambered up into the wide seat, laid her hands on the broad arms, and pretended she was a queen. "Which queen?" Aunt Clothilde had asked.

"Queen Marie Antoinette!" Suzanne had answered proudly. Uncle Bernard, who had been alive then, had chuckled and said that was impossible, for the chair was the wrong period.

"—Even though it is in any case a modern fake," Aunt Clothilde had put in.

"Oh, *is* it?" Suzanne had been disappointed to learn this. She preferred to think of the chair as a priceless antique.

"Better to choose the English Queen Victoria," Uncle Bernard had continued, "than a French tragedy queen."

"But Queen Victoria was so ugly!" Suzanne had complained, pouting her lower lip.

"Not when she was young," Uncle Bernard said; and he had made Suzanne look among her English coins to see if she had a penny with a profile of the young Victoria. . . .

But all that happened such a long time ago. Now Suzanne laid the bunch of flowers on the chair seat, a splash of bright color against the faded silk covering. Then she turned away from the closed door that would have been opened to her with such incredulous delight.

There was an atmosphere of calm in the anteroom to the Commandant's office at Gestapo Headquarters. Lieutenant Hoffman sat at his desk, looking through the list of suspects they hoped to round up in a raid on a Montmartre *bistro* the next day. Thanks to the information they had . . . extracted . . . from Henri the street artist, they should be able to make a clean sweep of that area. L'Escargot was obviously the meeting place of an important Resistance cell.

He glanced at his wristwatch. In seven and a half minutes, Corporal Schmidt was due for his briefing. Erich smiled. Who would have thought the corporal possessed such artistic talent? If he did his job convincingly enough, they should catch the bird in their net without difficulty. Then—and Lieutenant Hoffman straightened in his chair —there might well be promotion for the part he had played in this affair. After all, it was he who had first noticed the recurring pattern in the pavement display of pictures, as he passed by old Henri's pitch each day on his way to the office. Almost like a code, he'd thought idly. . . . Well, his hunch had been correct. They had pulled in the old man for questioning—and persuaded him to speak. Then they had shot him. Naturally, they had shot him; he was of no further use. But they had made one mistake. An over-zealous guard had violently trampled the street artist's canvas to pieces. It had happened before Lieutenant Hoffman could intervene. (Yet it was odd— that was the moment when the old man had given in and told them what they wanted to know. Was it because he saw his paintings destroyed?) They could have done with those paintings now. It would have saved a lot of trouble. There would have been no need to brief Corporal Schmidt. . . .

Hauptmann Hoffman. It sounded well.

There was the sound of approaching footsteps. Erich raised his fair head and set his expression. Corporal Schmidt appeared.

"I will tell the Commandant you are here."

The three of them—the Commandant, Lieutenant Hoffman, and Corporal Schmidt—went through the briefing together. The corporal was to take over the street artist's pitch for a day . . . two days . . . as long as necessary. Disguise would be easy enough; age, dirt, and rags presented no difficulties. The corporal was to paint six pictures. Erich had photographed each one just before Henri was arrested. Now he handed the color slides to the corporal, who held them to the light and studied them carefully.

"You will reproduce these—daubs—in exact detail," the Commandant ordered him. "They must be indistinguishable from the originals." His eyes retained the same expression all the time he was speaking, and, in this sense, they might have been described as expressionless. They betrayed nothing of his thoughts or feelings. He went on to enumerate the pictures, his voice expressing his contempt for the highly colored canvases: "The woodland glade; the seashore; the sunset over the valley with pine trees; the view of the Sacré Cœur; the Eiffel Tower; and the scene with the street café . . ."

Actually, the Commandant was something of an art connoisseur. At this time, he was arranging for several Impressionist paintings to be taken out of France for his collection of paintings in Germany. They were "gifts" from an eminent Jewish art dealer in Paris.

Corporal Schmidt found the expressionless eyes very disconcerting. He shifted his gaze away from them. "Very good, Herr Commandant."

The Commandant's mouth smiled slightly, but not his eyes. "If somebody comes along, puts twenty-five francs in your cap, and asks: 'Is the Eiffel Tower for sale?' you will reply—'If you can take it away with you.' This is a joke; there will be laughter." The Commandant paused. "Under cover of the laughter you will repeat this address —L'Escargot, Rue Gaulaincourt. Is this clear?"

"Perfectly, Herr Commandant."

"We will be watching you. Lieutenant Hoffman will be standing close by, close enough to hear what is said."

Corporal Schmidt stood to attention as he was dismissed. He had been provided with canvases and paints in a room overlooking a courtyard where they sometimes shot prisoners. He hoped there would be no shooting while he was painting; that would make it difficult to concentrate.

His pictures must be indistinguishable from the originals, the Commandant had said. Corporal Schmidt shivered as he recalled the Commandant's basilisk stare. The Commandant would be displeased if his paintings were not good enough. He might then decide to terminate his service in Paris. Corporal Schmidt had no wish to be transferred. The Army of the Reich was advancing now through Rumania. More and more troops were being sent east. They said there would be an attack on Russia soon.

It was pleasant, here in Paris. Soon it would be spring. The trees along the Seine would be in leaf. Paris in the spring! No, Corporal Schmidt certainly did not want to be transferred to the Eastern Front. And so—he must do this job well.

Clothilde Duchesne was listening to the radio. Her chair was drawn up before the old-fashioned wardrobe in her bedroom. The radio was inside the wardrobe, on the shelf where she kept spare blankets. If necessary, she could quickly throw a blanket over the set to conceal it from inquisitive eyes. The volume was turned low; she was listening to the broadcast from England, to the voice of "Major Britain."

". . . You are the unknown soldiers . . . a great silent army, waiting and watching . . ."

In every broadcast Major Britain encouraged the peoples of occupied Europe in their resistance against the German invader. His voice continued:

"The night is your friend. The V is your sign."

Then came the tapping of the V sign—V for Victory. Dot-dot-dot dash; dot-dot-dot dash . . .

Her radio was a great comfort to Madame Duchesne now that she was so much alone. Her son Raoul had escaped soon after the fall of France to join the Free French Army under de Gaulle. She did not know where he was; she prayed that he was alive still and that they would be reunited after the war. Mostly, she tried to keep to herself these days. It was the best plan. You could trust very few people. An indiscreet remark might be repeated, exaggerated, and reach the ears of the Germans. . . .

There were neighbors in the same apartment building, longstanding acquaintances of hers, whose views on the Occupation differed widely from her own. They shrugged their shoulders, ran down the Resistance movement, asked what was the use of working against the invader. France was defeated—it was sensible to make the best of a bad job, they said. If you got on the right side of the Germans, they weren't so bad . . . one should be philosophical about the situation.

Clothilde Duchesne thought of these people contemptuously. They were the sort who had not scrupled to bring the black market into existence. They could afford to buy real coffee, butter, eggs, at the inflated prices of scarcity,

and did not see why they should not make use of their
good fortune. They did not consider those less fortunate
than themselves, who either went without so many things
which until recently had been part of their daily life,
or else suffered great hardship in order to procure them.

And these neighbors, so devoted to their own skins,
certainly did not listen to the broadcasts from England.
They would not have heard that famous speech to the
French people made by Winston Churchill last October.
The British Prime Minister's words were a vivid memory
to Clothilde Duchesne. He had spoken from London in
the midst of the *blitzkrieg*. The London blitz . . . one
heard plenty about that in the German-censored news
bulletins on the French radio.

"Ici, dans cette ville de Londres," Mr. Churchill had
begun, *"que Herr Hitler prétend réduire en cendres et
que ses avions bombardent en ce moment, nos gens tiennent bon."* And he had continued, ironically: *"Nous
attendons l'invasion promis de longue date. Les poissons
aussi . . ."*

The fishes, too! Yes, it seemed that Hitler had indeed
abandoned his plan for the invasion of Britain. When he
pitted the strength of the *Luftwaffe* against the RAF last
summer, he had never reckoned on the loss of so many
crews and aircraft. The Battle of Britain had been a
decisive German defeat. The fighter planes of the RAF
had repulsed attack after attack by the *Luftwaffe*. And
the blitz on London and the other cities of Britain was
not having the effect the *Führer* had expected. The British, so far from losing their morale, had hardened their
resolve to win the war. In Mr. Churchill's words, *"nos
gens tiennent bon."* And in her heart, Clothilde Duchesne

knew this was true, in spite of the propaganda to the contrary put across by the Germans.

How were they in Renchester, she wondered. Her thoughts often went out to the house in St. Oswald's Terrace.

There were rumors that Hitler would soon turn his attention eastward, to Russia. Well, one emperor had met his downfall there, and had been compelled to make a disastrous retreat from Moscow. One must hope that Adolf Hitler would follow in the footsteps of Napoleon Bonaparte. . . .

As she got up to shut the wardrobe after the broadcast had finished, her glance fell on the vase of flowers by her bedside. Anemones. She wondered again who could have brought them to her door. She could think of no one in Paris close enough to know that these were the flowers she loved best. Suzanne used to have some sent to her by Interflora each year on her birthday. Suzanne . . . no, of course it was impossible. Crazy to think Suzanne might be in Paris! And yet—these were strange times. Madame Duchesne touched the delicate petals with her fingertips. Nothing was too fantastic to be true, these days.

Gone to Earth

C⟳⟳

A gang of workmen was removing the iron railings that ran the length of St. Oswald's Terrace. They were being taken away for scrap iron, to be used for munitions. At number eleven, Dr. Sinclair stood by his study window, staring out unseeingly. In his hand he held a letter he had received from the War Office.

One of the workmen noticed the figure at the window and nudged his mate. "Look at 'is face," he said. "'ad a shock, if yer ask me."

Dr. Sinclair glanced at the letter again, though he already knew it by heart. "Your daughter was recently sent out of this country on a Special Mission. . . . We regret to inform you that the date set for her return has now expired. . . . Should any further information come to hand, we will not hesitate to get in touch with you."

Suzanne—Special Mission! He could scarcely believe it. He tried to recall the details of her last visit home. She had always been so vague and unforthcoming about her work in London; he had assumed this was because it wasn't particularly interesting. Now he realized that his daughter had been extremely careful not to divulge just how interesting it was. He remembered a letter in which she had said she was going to be out of London for a while. . . . He had imagined her office was moving temporarily to the suburbs; he'd felt relieved she would have a respite from the London blitz. If only he'd known!

In his younger days, Vernon Sinclair had been an avid reader of Zane Gray, Edgar Wallace, Conan Doyle. He'd reveled in tales of the Foreign Legion and romances of espionage. (Since then, his reading taste had narrowed into a steady stream of green-backed Penguin detective stories; they were his late-night sedative.) He found it incredible that Suzanne, his daughter, should be mixed up in that sort of thing! It was a double shock: that official-sounding phrase—"the date set for her return has now expired" repeated itself over and over in his mind. He passed his hand across his eyes and turned away from the window, feeling old.

Before nightfall, the workmen drove away with the final lorry-load of railings from St. Oswald's Terrace. Suzzane would have missed the spiky iron palings, had she suddenly turned the corner and walked along the pavement to the front door of number eleven. They had been there as long as she could remember.

"Marie Clavion" made her final visit to Montmartre on the last day in January.

1941. Already, this new year showed significant developments in the pattern of the war. The British army in the Western Desert was advancing on Tobruk. On

New Year's Day, Joseph Stalin, leader of the U.S.S.R., had declared, "Russia must hold herself in readiness to face her enemies." President Roosevelt had ordered the United States navy to be brought up to war strength, a gesture to which Hitler responded by threatening to torpedo American ships. In terms of money, the war was now costing Britain ten million, five hundred thousand pounds each day.

As usual, Suzanne had made sure there was a twenty-five franc piece in her purse. Each time, she went to Montmartre by a different route, crossing the Seine by another bridge, taking short cuts through new streets. After each of her previous visits to the quarter, she had gone into the church of St. Pierre, close by the Sacré Cœur. Here she had rested, and prayed for guidance. Here, too, her thoughts often turned to her father. They informed your next-of-kin if you failed to keep a rendezvous. He would be very worried about her. She never stayed very long in the church. Churches in Paris were unheated this winter, cold places in which to linger.

Today, January sunshine touched the white dome of the Sacré Cœur. Suzanne slackened her steps as she approached the entrance to the arcade in the Rue Gabrielle. She could see the old artist huddled in his rags. A young man in a tweed overcoat stood close by him, studying a shop window that displayed rosaries, plaster statuettes of the Holy Family, religious prints, devotional books.

She loitered past the familiar canvases propped against the wall of the arcade. The painting she had looked for so many times in vain seemed to jump out at her.

The Eiffel Tower! She stopped, opened her purse,

took out the twenty-five francs, and dropped the coin into the shabby cap that lay on the ground beside the old artist. But her aim was not true; the coin rolled along the ground. The artist stretched out a grimy hand and recovered it deftly, nodding his thanks.

Est-ce-que le Tour Eiffel à vendre, mon vieux?—the words were already formed in her mind. But Suzanne did not say them. She hesitated, her thoughts racing wildly. And among them was the intuitive notion that perhaps the man in the tweed coat, looking in the shop window, half-turned towards her, was waiting to hear her say just that.

What made her hold back the words? This. She had once seen someone else toss the old artist a coin, and that too had rolled away. He had reached out to pick it up; but his hand shook so much that he only managed to get hold of the coin with difficulty.

Henri Legaux (in the far-off days when he was a student who showed some promise, people used to address him by name, instead of calling him merely *"mon vieux"* or "old Henri") had long since learned to console himself for his failure by means of the absinthe bottle. It was years since he had been able to wield a paintbrush, his hands shook so uncontrollably. The paintings he used to exhibit had been painted a long time ago. And it was this shaking of the hands that Suzanne had noticed.

If this were not the same man—if it were someone posing in the old artist's place—why, then, it was not difficult for Suzanne to draw the conclusion. She glanced at the familiar pictures again: the woodland glade with the emerald-green grass; the white-crested waves of the seashore; the brilliant sunset over the pine trees; the

view of the Sacré Cœur, looking like an enormous in-
verted pudding-basin; the Eiffel Tower; the street café.
... Surely there was something—unfamiliar—about them.
In the old days, she had often seen students at their
easels in the Louvre, copying famous paintings. They
reproduced the original faithfully; every fold in a gar-
ment, every shadow in the background. But the result
was—a copy. And these daubs in the arcade: they were
copies, too—she was sure of it.

These thoughts passed through her mind in a few
seconds. Then her decision was made. She sauntered on
to the end of the arcade, emerged into the street, then
walked across the Place St. Pierre. She wanted to hurry,
but knew that she must not walk too quickly. She felt
as if a dreaded nightmare, the sort from which one always wakes just in time, had been extended into reality.
She was aware that the man in the tweed coat was following her. She must try to shake him off. It wouldn't
be easy. She planned her route in her mind. Whatever
happened, she mustn't return to Marcel's shop. She would
try to get to Neuilly . . . she had already started on the
first lap of her escape route.

Down a small street that led into the Rue Dancourt;
into the Boulevard de Clichy. . . . There were more
people here; perhaps she could lose her shadower in the
crowd. Over the road, into the Place Pigalle, then on in
the direction of the Gare St. Lazare. . . . But he was always there, a few yards behind her; just across the street;
turning the last corner. . . .

Now she had reached the busy station approach. German army vehicles were everywhere, filled with soldiers
and supplies. She made her way into the station, thread-

ing a path through the trucks, risking being run down several times in her urgent need to shake off the pursuer. A feeling of desperation seized her. She fought it as she walked along to the entrance to the Métro. She went down the steps, hurriedly bought a ticket at the kiosk. She seemed to be safe at last! But, as she turned to pass through the barrier, she saw out of the tail of her eye a figure coming down the Métro steps. . . . With a sick sense of despair, she waited on the platform. There was nowhere else to run. She was trapped underground, like an animal that had gone to earth only to be ferreted out by the hunter.

The muffled roar of an approaching train brought with it a gust of warm, dusty air and a bouquet of garlic and Gaulois cigarettes. . . .

Lieutenant Hoffman had not been sure until he reached the Gare St. Lazare. Standing in the arcade, his gaze apparently fixed on the plaster statuettes and gilt-framed prints in the shop window, he had not thought it possible that this girl could be the agent they were expecting. A typical French girl, a Parisienne—dark, simply dressed, with a certain style. . . . He imagined she was a business girl returning to her office after the lunch hour. Then she had stopped, and thrown down the twenty-five franc piece. And—he could have sworn it—she very nearly spoke the words he was waiting to hear. They had seemed to hang in the air. But after a second or two, she had walked on, and he had been left with nothing but a hunch that she was the agent old Henri had been told would come to collect the information he had. So he acted on his hunch, and set off in Suzanne's footsteps.

But—he was not sure until he reached the station. And then, as he followed the slim, dark-haired girl along to the entrance to the Métro, something clicked in his mind. He remembered an October day three years ago. Crewe Station, England! He had been on his way to the provincial town where he had combined some business research with his espionage work. And walking ahead of him as he changed trains had been a slim, dark-haired girl who walked just so . . . *the same girl.* Fantastic! Oh, yes, it was fantastic. But there was no mistake. This girl was a British agent.

He quickened his pace, and started down the Métro steps just as she turned away from the ticket kiosk. He hurried on towards the platform barrier, elated by the success of the whole operation. Yesterday's raid on L'Escargot had gone off according to plan. Two leaders of the Resistance cell had been captured. The Commandant had been pleased. He would be better pleased still to know that the British agent had been traced. *Hauptmann* Hoffman! Yes, it sounded well. . . .

Quite suddenly, Lieutenant Hoffman tripped and sprawled full-length, twisting his ankle violently. He lay dazed for some moments, then tried to get up. But it was no good; his right leg would not bear his weight.

It was old Mimi's most successful trip to date; she had never achieved a broken leg before. They had to bring a stretcher and an ambulance to take the lieutenant away. "A Gestapo man!" she boasted afterwards. "I recognized him even though he wasn't in uniform, with that nasty black spider they call a swastika on his arm! It's the way they walk, the way they look—oh, yes, I can smell a

Gestapo man a kilometer away! And he was after someone, I could tell. Well, I put pain to his sport!"

That was how Erich Hoffman lost his quarry in the
Paris Underground . . . and how Suzanne managed to
reach Neuilly safely, and start on the hazardous journey
to Spain.

The blame for the unsuccessful outcome of this little
adventure fell chiefly on Corporal Schmidt. Obviously,
his paintings had not been good enough. They had failed
to deceive the agent. Quite soon afterwards, he was
ordered to the Eastern Front; in June, he played his
part in Germany's great attack on Russia, along a 1,500-
mile front that stretched from Finland to the Black
Sea. Corporal Schmidt never saw Paris in the spring,
after all.

The Thousandth Day

Spring, 1942: three people were working in a field which the tractor had furrowed like an acre of brown corduroy. There was Mary, lately maid-of-all-work at number 8 Laburnum Crescent, now tanned and buxom in her Land Army uniform of fawn jodhpurs and green jersey. There was Angelo, who a short while ago had been fighting for *Il Duce* in North Africa—until, to his great relief, he was captured by the British Eighth Army and sent to England as a P.O.W. He was out of his element in this English landscape of muddy fields beneath a mackerel sky: he should have been tilling his father's vineyard on a terraced hillside in Campania. The third field worker was James Hartley, who had fought and won his own private battle as a conscientious objector. He used to be one of Arnold Beaton's assistants; he had chosen architecture as his profession because there was something in him that urged him to create and forbade him to destroy.

It took courage—a certain brand of courage—to make your stand as a "conshie." You had to prove that your objection to taking an active part in the war, to being called up into one of the services, was genuinely based on moral grounds, that you were not merely shirking your duty. Then you were directed into noncombatant work.

During the last two years, Jim Hartley had grown used to the averted eyes of former friends who *would* not understand his feelings, and to the barely concealed contempt of people like Mary, who *could* not understand the way he felt. At least no one sent out white feathers now as they had during the 1914 war. . . . A few of the people he knew understood his motives, even sympathized with them. Arnold Beaton was one. Esmé Beaton was another. But there were few Rencastrians as open-minded as that. Jim Hartley was fond of Esmé. They used to see quite a lot of each other before she went to London.

As they worked, each of the three was occupied with his own thoughts. Those of Angelo and Mary overlapped. Angelo admired Mary as she worked, her green jersey strained over her ample breasts, her face flushed with exertion. Mary, aware of his admiration and pleased by it, wondered if it would be all right to walk out with an Eytie. The other girls in the village would gossip, but why should she care about that? They gossiped, whomever you walked out with. Half of them had their eyes on Angelo, anyway. After all, it wasn't as if he was fighting against England now—he was actually helping in the war effort, working on the farm. She straightened her back for a moment's rest and glanced scornfully at

Jim. At least Angelo had played a man's part in the war. . . .

Jim's thoughts were more impersonal. He was recalling the words of God's promise to Noah, which he had once learned as a small boy in Sunday school.

How did it go? "While the earth remaineth, seedtime and harvest, and cold and heat, and summer and winter, and day and night shall not cease." Now, at this time when patriotic propaganda debased the truth; when the instincts of a murderer could be translated as "courage" on the battlefield; when medals were struck as the currency of that false virtue—now it was a reassurance to work on the land. Seedtime and harvest—cold and heat —summer and winter—day and night: these constant things were very close when you tilled the soil. Jim smiled. The introduction of double summertime to give the farmers an extra hour of daylight might, he supposed, be regarded as a minor alteration to day and night. . . .

He looked up automatically as the drone of a plane came through the layers of feathery sky. There had been few air raids recently, and land-workers had grown casual about taking their tin hats into the fields with them. Once, last summer, they had all scrambled into a ditch to escape being machine-gunned by a lone Messerschmidt. The airplane came down through the cloud and swooped low over the field. It was not English; at the sight of its unfamiliar markings, Angelo jerked his head back uneasily and with his eyes measured the distance to the nearest hedge.

Jim reassured him. "Americano," he said, screwing up his eyes to gaze into the clouds. "Dakota."

The plane droned out of sight, trailing a white slip

stream that mingled with the cloud patterns. The pilot headed for his new base in England, and the brown corduroy field with its three oddly assorted workers was left far behind.

"America is at her battle stations," President Roosevelt had declared in October, 1941. All that autumn, the world wondered when she would commit herself to war. Then the decision was forced upon her. At dawn on Sunday, December 7, three hundred and fifty Japanese bombers swooped upon the United States Pacific Fleet as it rode at anchor in the Hawaiian Island base of Pearl Harbor.

Pearl Harbor: an exotic name, conjuring up images of blue lagoons and dusky native girls in grass skirts. No defenses were prepared at Pearl Harbor; the attack was totally unexpected. When the Japanese planes vanished over the horizon once more, only one American battleship remained. The rest of the fleet was destroyed.

Pearl Harbor: a place of sunken ships and sudden death. So Japan gained the mastery of the Pacific—and, by means of a stroke more outrageous than the most farfetched episode in any novel, the story of the war entered a new chapter.

The United States and Britain immediately declared war on Japan. Four days later, Germany and Italy declared war on the United States.

Now war had spread like a heath fire to every part of the world. In Europe, the few countries that remained neutral—Spain, Portugal, Switzerland, Sweden—stood like pockets of grassland perilously preserved in the midst of the encircling flames.

The war in the Far East moved quickly. For some time, Japanese troops had been massing in Indo-China. In the third week of December, they invaded Hong Kong, and on Christmas Day the British garrison surrendered. This disaster was followed by Japanese advances in the Philippines and Malaya, by the surrender of Singapore in February, and the invasion of Sumatra, Borneo, New Guinea, Java, and Burma. India was threatened; and Tojo, the Japanese Premier, warned Australia that Japan was determined "to destroy the influence of Great Britain and America."

Meanwhile, there was dramatic action in the Western Desert. During the spring of 1941, Hitler had sent the Deutsche Afrika Korps, under the command of General Rommel, to the rescue of the shattered Italian forces in North Africa. Fierce fighting resulted in a British retreat: only Tobruk, with its important harbor, held out. Rommel's forces were at the frontiers of Egypt. Then, in November, the British Eighth Army crossed the Libyan frontier and after a tremendous tank battle, relieved Tobruk. Ken Martin was among those troops in the garrison at Tobruk who cheered themselves hoarse as the men of the Eighth Army, with their New Zealand comrades, rode through the streets. Ken spent Christmas Day that year in blazing sunshine, with the smell of burning tanks in his nostrils: a far cry from Christmas Day in Povey Street, overfed with turkey and plum pudding, the family sitting around the dinner table in crepe-paper hats.

The following month, Rommel launched a counter-attack, and the hard-won British gains were lost. By May, the British forces had retreated to the Alamein Line, only forty miles from Alexandria and a hundred miles from Cairo. It seemed very likely that the Axis would achieve their ambition to invade Egypt, after all. Rommel, promoted to Field Marshal, pressed on towards Tobruk.

In Russia, the German forces, caught in the icy grip of winter, were slowly being forced back. Corporal Schmidt, late of the Occupation force in Paris, was one among thousands of German soldiers who perished from exposure to the merciless blizzards.

As a result of the United States' entry into the war, London was "invaded" in 1942. American soldiers, sailors, and airmen, based in Britain or on leave from active service, spent their leisure time in London, their uniforms mingling in the streets with those from a score of other allied countries—so many different kinds that someone was reputed to have walked down Piccadilly, for a bet, in the uniform of a German General, and remained un-detected.

In May that year, Pauline Stanford, now a Leading Wren, was posted to Greenwich for an advanced signals course. One morning, finding herself with a free day, she decided to explore London. Her previous visits had always been hurried, mostly en route to some other destination. She took a train to Charing Cross, and began her sightseeing in Trafalgar Square. School holidays had begun, and children were feeding the plump-breasted pigeons that perched clumsily on their outstretched arms. No food rationing for them! Pauline thought.

Men and women in uniform strolled around in the May sunshine, chattering and laughing. Everyone seemed to have a companion; in the midst of the crowd Pauline felt lonely. It would have been pleasant to share her day with someone. The only person she knew in London was Esmé Beaton. But Esmé would be working during the day. Pauline thought she might telephone her later, and perhaps go to see her that evening. She remembered how they had once planned to share a flat together in London, she and Esmé. Funny how things had turned out otherwise!

In spite of bombs and shellfire, Nelson stood unflinching on his column in the center of Trafalgar Square, flanked by Landseer's stone lions. Pauline shaded her eyes with one hand to look up at him. She was wearing her WRNS uniform and suddenly felt absurdly symbolic, as though she and Nelson were the subject of a Landseer picture—"The Call to Duty" would be an appropriate title, she thought with amusement, recollecting Nelson's famous last signal. . . .

"What's the joke, sister?"

An American voice broke across her thoughts. She turned, her look of amusement giving way to a frosty stare. Several crushing retorts sprang to her mind; but they remained unspoken. For somehow it was obvious that the young American G.I. who had made that remark had steeled himself to do so in order to get into conversation with her. He looked almost apologetic. He looked very young, too, with sandy-colored hair that stood up in close-cropped spikes all over his head. Pauline had noticed that most of the American G.I.s wore their hair this way.

So, to her own surprise, she smiled at him. "I was thinking about Lord Nelson," she said. "Not," she added, "that I consider him a joke—" She decided that her reflections were too complicated to explain in a second to a stranger.

" 'England expects each man this day to do his duty,' " the American quoted solemnly. "I learned that in a history book at school. Lord Nelson was a great guy. That sure was a cunning trick he made with the telescope, putting it to his blind eye. Horatio Nelson and Winston S. Churchill—two great Britishers."

Pauline, being English, felt vaguely responsible for both Nelson and Churchill, and was gratified. She asked: "Is this the first time you've been in London?"

The American nodded. "The very first time," he repeated, slurring his r's in a way that Pauline found fascinating.

"I don't know London either," she told him. "I'm spending the day sightseeing."

The American looked astonished. "But gee—England's so *small*—such a *little* country. How come you never got to London before?"

"Well—I've always lived three hundred-odd miles away!"

This did not impress the G.I. "Only three hundred miles? Why, that's nothing. Where I live, it's five hundred miles to the nearest big city—San Francisco. We think nothing of driving there to visit with friends. But you seem to think of London the way we think of New York. Come to think of it, New York is the same distance from San Francisco as it is from London. Gee, that's quite a thought!"

Pauline felt overwhelmed by distance. "It must seem to you as though the enemy is just around the corner," she remarked, "considering it's only twenty-one miles across the English Channel!"

The young American grinned. "You're right there, it does. Say," he went on, "what's your name?"

"Pauline. Pauline Stanford."

"Pauline. That's a pretty name. I'm Spike—Spike Rodgers."

"Spike." Pauline's eyes widened as she repeated the name. Well, it was a change from the Johns and Tonys and Bills of Renchester Tennis Club. . . .

His name suited Spike. He was tall and lean—"rangy" was the adjective that best described him, Pauline thought. She didn't quite know what that meant, but she had seen it used to describe film stars who played cowboys on the screen. And Spike's blue eyes looked as though they were used to scanning those long distances he talked about.

"Well, now we're acquainted, Pauline, how say we look around the sights together? I was feeling pretty lonesome until I met you. It'll be more fun being rubbernecks together."

"Rub—rubbernecks?" Pauline looked startled.

"Isn't that what you call someone who looks around the sights?"

"Oh. We call them sightseers—or tourists. But I *like* rubbernecks! It's much more expressive."

Spike laughed. "I guess there're many things we say that seem like a foreign language to you Britishers. I got talking one time to some guy in a public house, and, boy, was he interested to learn I drove my auto back home on *gas*! I couldn't figure what he was so excited about—until I realized that what we call gasoline, you call petrol. I guess that guy reckoned he was going to beat the petrol rationing!" Spike paused and looked at Pauline. "Well now—how about it? Are we going rub— . . . ah, sightseeing together?"

He looked a bit like a pleading Airedale. Pauline hesitated only a moment. After all, she had been feeling lonesome too. And Spike seemed a nice guy. His American way of talking was catching! She smiled warmly.

"O.K."

Spike beamed. "That's swell. Let's go!" He paused. "*Where'll* we go?"

There was something in his voice that gave Pauline the impression he had a special place fixed in his mind, but was too shy to say so. She wondered what it was. Buckingham Palace? The non-stop revue at the Windmill? St. Paul's Cathedral? The Cockney street market in Petticoat Lane?

"You decide, Spike."

"Well—you may think this is silly." He ran the fingers of one hand through his crew cut, making his hair spikier than ever. "But I'd sure like to visit the Zoological Gardens in Regent's Park." He pronounced the words very carefully as though they really were part of a foreign language.

"The Zoo! That's a splendid idea."

Spike beamed happily. "I suppose we should really go see some place of historic interest," he said cheerfully as he escorted Pauline across the road to a bus bound for Camden Town.

Pauline felt almost as though she were taking out a

small boy for a treat. "We ought to have a bag of buns
for the elephants," she remarked as they clambered onto
the top deck of the bus.

During their tour of the Zoo, Pauline learned something of Spike Rodgers' background. He belonged to a
small town, smaller than Renchester. "What you'd call
a one-horse town, I guess," he told her. He'd enlisted
in the army soon after leaving high school; until now
his world had been made up of teenage high-school
society—gatherings in the drug store, with cokes and
slangy backchat; vacations at summer camp by a lakeside,
with days spent fishing; dating girls for football games
and dances at the country club, and necking in the car
afterwards because that was what everybody else in the
group did.

Spike had as little notion of the British way of life as
Pauline had of his outlook on the world. He was as
ignorant of the forms that British class-consciousness
took, for example, as Pauline was of the taboos and crazes
of the teenage group to which Spike had belonged back
home, with their saddle shoes and Scotch-tartan skirts,
their cowboy jeans and checkered shirts.

Some of the animals from the London Zoo had been
sent to the country branch at Whipsnade for safety; careful plans had been made in case any of those that were
left should escape as a result of bomb damage.

"Imagine a cobra at large!" Pauline shuddered in the
dim light of the reptile house, where Spike felt bold
enough to take hold of her hand.

There was an uneasiness about looking at creatures
confined in cages. Some—the lions, for instance—were
sufficiently dignified almost to convince you that they

were there especially to gaze at you. But others, such as
the sad-eyed wolf, restlessly pacing his cage, were merely
prisoners.

"I guess it's pretty much the same as being a prisoner
of war," Spike commented when Pauline told him these
thoughts. "You get food and shelter, but if you try to
escape, they shoot you."

Standing by the man-made rocks and caves and arti-
ficial pools of Mappin Terrace, they watched two polar
bears playing about in the water.

"They have themselves a pretty good time, anyhow,"
Spike said, "fooling around in a swimming hole all day."

Some other visitors came and stood beside Pauline and
Spike: an elegant woman, an elderly Nanny, and two
rather repressed-looking children in tweed coats with velvet collars. Their mother looked bored, the Nanny anxious,
and the two children had little personality beyond the
neatness of their well-cut coats and clean woollen gloves.

The little boy had evidently been working out an elab-
orate joke ever since they'd passed by the mountain goats.
"You're a goat, Nanny, and we're your kids," he snig-
gered. But no one took any notice.

"Give the bears their treacle, Nanny," drawled the
mother.

"Don't you see, don't you see—goats and kids, *nanny-
goats!*" shrilled the little boy.

"Hush, Colin, that's not very polite to Nanny," his
mother said with a frown.

To her amazement, Pauline saw the Nanny produce
a two-pound tin of golden syrup from her hold-all. She
prised up the lid with a coin, and threw it into the bears'
enclosure.

Even Spike whistled softly. "Say, I thought you were short on sugar over here," he murmured.

"We are," Pauline replied grimly. "You should see my little sister tucking into her sweet ration each month. Three-quarters of a pound isn't all that much to stretch over four weeks."

The two children were more animated now, watching one of the huge bears balance the tin on its nose to try to lick out the syrup.

Somehow, Pauline didn't think that these opulent-looking visitors had saved up their rations for a visit to the Zoo. On the contrary, they were the sort who got as much as they could on the black market. Thank goodness, Britain was free of really large-scale trafficking of that sort, Pauline thought. There were rumors that in Occupied France and other Continental countries, you had to deal on the black market or starve.

Mappin Terrace completed their circuit of the Zoo. There was a telephone box near the bus stop outside, and Pauline slipped inside to telephone Esmé. She had decided that she'd had enough of Spike all to herself. For one thing, she didn't want to progress any farther than the handholding.

Esmé sounded really pleased to hear Pauline was in London. "Yes, come round and spend the evening here," she urged. "We can have a good gossip about Renchester and the old folks at home."

"Actually"—Pauline hesitated—"actually, I've been spending the day with a boy friend."

"What, Clive Mawton?"

"Oh, no!"—carelessly Pauline brushed aside the thought

of Clive. "An American. A G.I. He's called Spike, believe it or not."

"Well—bring Spike with you!" Esmé sounded amused.

"Who was that?" Lorna asked as Esmé, smiling, turned away from the telephone. She was unpacking her briefcase, having just got home from work. "Look," she said, "oranges. I joined a queue at a shop in the Strand— I had to go that way to arrange about some costumes for a production of *Antony and Cleopatra* that's going out to the Middle East. Only had to wait half an hour. Aren't they gorgeous! Who'd ever have thought we'd be so thrilled to see an orange!"

Esmé looked suitably impressed. "That was a girl from my home town on the telephone," she said. "Pauline Stanford. I was smiling because it sounds as though she's picked up a G.I. called Spike—and, somehow, I can't imagine her doing anything so outrageous! She was always the sort of girl who wore cashmere twin-sets— you'll see what I mean when you meet her. Funnily enough, we once half planned to share a flat together. I'm sure it would have been a great mistake—she's not really my type at all. Anyway, she—and Spike—are both coming round later on."

"That makes two of Uncle Sam's nephews," Lorna said. "Andy MacIntyre's coming this evening too—he's just back from a training course. You know he's joined the United States Air Force? It'll be nice to see him again."

And "nice" was a big understatement, so far as Lorna was concerned.

The evening was a great success. Spike and Pauline had a meal at a Lyons Corner House (all restaurant meals were limited now to five shillings a head), and arrived at the Chelsea flat to find Andy MacIntyre telling Esmé and Lorna about his first experiences as a pilot.

". . . so I came down through the cloud to find out where I was," he was saying, "and nearly hit a plowed field. There were three people in it—I was so low I could see the whites of their eyes. Were they scared! So was I!"

He grinned, and turned to greet the new arrivals.

"Spike picked me up in the shadow of Lord Nelson," Pauline said cheerfully, introducing him.

Goodness, how you've changed, Esmé thought. The Pauline she'd known in Renchester would never have made that remark. WRNS uniform suited her, too, better than a cashmere twin-set.

In the course of the evening, Lorna was dismayed to realize that Andy was attracted by Pauline.

"By the way," Pauline remarked to Esmé at one point, when Lorna had started playing the inevitable gramophone records, "have you heard about Suzanne Sinclair? You know, Dr. Sinclair's daughter, who used to teach at the High School?"

"Yes, I know," Esmé said quietly.

"Well, it's all very mysterious, but she hasn't been seen or heard of for *months*. Dr. Sinclair came to see Mummy the other day, and apparently he just shut up like a clam when she asked about Suzanne. I thought perhaps you might know what had happened to her. She was supposed to be working in London."

Esmé looked embarrassed. She knew more than she could tell, for Gordon had confided in her after visiting

Suzanne's father three months ago. At first, he had come to see Esmé because he was so anxious and needed the relief of confiding his anxiety. But as the weeks, then months, slipped by, the image of Suzanne had receded. Esmé was gradually taking her place in his affections. She and Gordon were seeing a good deal of each other nowadays. The situation was a difficult one for Esmé, who at times almost felt that she was a usurper.

"How odd," she said now to Pauline. "I—I wonder what could have happened to her."

Pauline noticed Esmé's embarrassment. And suddenly she remembered that ages ago, Esmé had had a crush on a young doctor—Gordon someone-or-other—whom everyone had thought Suzanne would marry. She recalled how Esmé had once asked her if she thought it would be all right to send him a Christmas card, and whether she ought to write inside it "with love from Esmé" or simply "from Esmé." . . . But surely she'd forgotten all about that by now! It had been only a schoolgirl crush, after all. Puzzled, Pauline turned to listen to Andy, who had just made a discovery.

"Listen, everyone! This is the thousandth day of the war! We ought to write a song about it. The twenty-ninth of May, nineteen hundred and forty-two . . ."

Lorna went into the kitchen and returned with a bowl of oranges. "We can commemorate it by eating these," she said. "Won by me. The fruits of victory." She sighed, and added: "No one ever commemorated the thousandth day of peace."

Andy glanced at her, surprised. He didn't associate Lorna with serious thoughts; she was labeled in his affections as an amusing girl to date—that was all. If he hadn't happened to meet Pauline that evening, Lorna's remark might have made him begin to see her with new eyes. But—he had met Pauline.

Before the party broke up, he asked Pauline if he could get in touch with her. "I've a few days' leave," he said. "I'd like to see you again—very much."

Though they had been aware of each other's presence all evening, this was the first time they had spoken closely. Pauline knew she must see him again. "Meet Andy MacIntyre," Esmé had said casually—but meeting him hadn't been like seeing a stranger for the first time: it had been more like recognizing someone she'd been searching for. Of course, they must see each other again; Pauline almost felt there was no choice in the matter. They exchanged telephone numbers, and soon afterwards she left the party with Spike, for she had to catch a train back to Greenwich.

She and Spike parted at the entrance to Charing Cross station, close to the place where they had met that morning.

"It's been a nice day," Pauline told him. "I'm glad we spent it together."

"When do we see each other again?" As he echoed Andy MacIntyre's wish, Spike looked like a pleading Airedale again. Pauline hated to hurt him. But she had to. It was no use pretending she wanted to see him again. She'd enjoyed the day in his company—but that was all.

"I—I shan't be at Greenwich much longer," she hedged. "After my course is finished I'll be posted back at Portsmouth."

"You know how I feel about distances in England!" Spike tried to make this sound lighthearted.

"Well—who knows, we may bump into each other again, just as we did this morning." Pauline attempted to keep up a bantering tone.

Then Spike dropped all the pretense. "O.K., Pauline, if that's the way you want it, I guess this is where we say good-by. It's been—nice—knowing you." He paused, looking disappointed and puzzled. Pauline felt hateful. "They told me English girls were kind of reserved," Spike went on, "but I thought you—well, you were real friendly towards me."

Pauline knew it was impossible to try to explain her feelings. She would only hurt him further. "I really did enjoy our day," she repeated. "Honestly. It was—swell!" She smiled, and started to walk away. "Good-by, Spike. Good luck!"

Then she hurried onto the crowded platform to await her train, with thoughts of Andy filling her mind. She didn't look round to see Spike still standing where she had left him, one arm half raised in a gesture of farewell.

After everyone had left, Esmé lay in the bath and conducted a conversation through the open bathroom door with Lorna, who was clearing up the sitting room.

"It's a good thing Gordon was on duty this evening and couldn't come," she said. "Pauline asked me about Suzanne. It would have been even more awkward than it was if he'd been here."

She tried to submerge herself in the five inches of bath water which the Government recommended as the maximum depth in order to conserve water supplies. People who were extra-patriotic even painted a Plimsoll line around the inside of their baths as a reminder. Why five inches and not six? Esmé wondered idly. She imagined some gigantic problem like those in the arithmetic textbooks: If all the baths in England are filled to a depth of five inches, how much water is required?

In the sitting room, Lorna emptied ashtrays. "What are you going to do about Gordon?" she asked.

"I could marry him, I know. I want to, and I feel that he'll ask me soon. I hope that doesn't sound calculating; it isn't meant to. But there's this awful question hanging over our relationship the whole time—at least, it is from my point of view. *What happens if Suzanne comes back?* I even feel that I'm sort of—betraying—her by saying 'if' instead of 'when.' How would Gordon react to seeing her again? That's what I want to know."

Lorna made sure the blackout at the window was properly secured. One night last week, the local warden on his rounds had shouted down at them from the street —"Put that light out!"

"You're afraid his feelings for you might change? And you imagine Suzanne might be in love with him?" she asked.

"That's it in a nutshell, m'dear. It's a two-edged question. Gordon asked Suzanne to marry him several times —he's told me that. But she refused. I don't *think* she did—does—love him. But of course I can't be sure."

She got out of the bath and draped herself in a towel. Lorna appeared in the doorway.

"Bath water still hot?" she asked. "If I add my five inches to yours, that makes ten. What a wallow!" She turned on the hot tap. "You know," she said, "it's pretty obvious to me (oh, how obvious these things always are to outsiders) that Gordon has been almost over-loyal to

Suzanne in the past. Honestly, Esmé, she had her chance to marry him if she wanted to. She turned it down. It's really quite simple. You mustn't confuse the issue because she's suddenly been revealed as a sort of heroine, and is—temporarily, we all hope—prevented from returning to England to clear up this tangle herself. I'm sure she would clear it up, you know. I'm positive she'd give you and Gordon her blessing."

Esmé frowned. "If only I could be *sure*. Oh, if only this horrible war would end! People's lives don't mark time—there's no hiatus in living, even though our way of life is interrupted. I'd like to marry Gordon *now*. I don't want to have to wait until I can be sure about Suzanne. Who said 'All's fair in love and war'? Someone absolutely batty. Love and war combined are the most fearful combination ever invented."

"I suspect there's always an element of doubt in this business of being in love—wartime or not," Lorna said slowly. "Always some chance, some risk, you've got to take in establishing a relationship. It asks a sort of—courage. And if Gordon asks you to marry him," she went on firmly, "that's surely sufficient proof for you that he's in love with you and no one else. He's not the sort of man to enter into marriage lightly. If he were, he'd have found someone else instead of Suzanne ages ago . . . the first time she refused him. Now go away and take your heartache with you! I want to enjoy my ten inches in peace!"

Esmé and Lorna always ended any discussion of the things nearest their hearts on a flippant note as though they were returning safely to familiar territory after a dangerous expedition. It was usually the things nearest

Esmé's heart which they discussed, however. Lorna was far more reserved.

As she lay in her unpatriotically deep bath, she thought about her own problem of the evening, about Andy's obvious admiration for Pauline Stanford. Being Lorna, she pondered it for a while, then sighed. Platitudes of self-consolation sprang to her mind, and she selected one at random. "What will be will be," she told herself; then added another to make weight: "No use crying over spilled milk."

A Name Faintly Written

On June 20, the Germans recaptured Tobruk and took prisoner twenty-five thousand men of the British Eighth Army. Ken Martin, who had survived one battle for Tobruk, was killed in this new struggle for the city. He was a part of the ugly wreckage of men and equipment that disfigured the Western Desert: the shattered bodies, the twisted metal of tanks and guns and trucks.

The battle continued; by the end of June, Rommel's armored columns had thrust over the frontier of Egypt. The original purpose for which the British attack in Libya had been launched—to defend Egypt from enemy invasion—was defeated. Rommel had succeeded in wresting the advantage from the Eighth Army. The British were forced back west of El Alamein.

When the official telegram announcing the death of Lance-Corporal Kenneth Martin, 1453581, arrived at the house in Povey Street, Eva received the news without an outward show of grief. She had been prepared for this ever since her wedding day. She knew that her loneliness now was shared by hundreds of other women whose experience of widowhood was to be far longer than their joy in married life. There were so many other couples, who, like Ken and Eva, had planned to make cosy homes in the future; had danced together at the local Palais; held hands in the ninepennies as they made their weekly escape into the celluloid dreamworld of the close-up embrace, the spangled dance routine, the luxurious restaurant interior where the leading man and the leading lady sipped champagne—and had then been plunged into this world of war. They had married, defying the nightmare that had crept upon them, and now their dreamworlds were faded forever.

Eva continued with her daily work at the munitions factory, though now she did not join in the chatter of workbench and canteen so easily. Life was strangely empty without Ken's closely written letters to look forward to and read over again; without the hoping for the time when they would see each other again. The popular songs relayed through the factory to keep up morale— music while they worked—were cheerless to Eva's ears. "We'll meet again," crooned Vera Lynn; "don't know where, don't know when—But I *know* we'll meet again some sunny day."

Beyond their first shocked exclamations and commiseration, the rest of the Gray family did not discuss Ken's death. It would be for Eva herself to recall him to their minds, later on, when she could think of him without such heavy grief as she now felt. Her mother was disapproving of the fact that she did not wear mourning. But Ken had liked her to wear bright colors; he always said that dark clothes were for old women.

Marion felt awkward in the presence of her sister's contained sorrow. However, in the crowded little house in Povey Street, it was easy enough to avoid close contact with any one member of her family alone—especially as she now spent three evenings a week at the Technical College, studying for the second part of the Chartered Auctioneers' Intermediate Exam. She had passed the first part, and was now immersed in the intricacies of receiverships and mortgages, which she must know in order to qualify for the Urban Section.

She could tell that Mr. Stanford was impressed by her industry—though he'd said something a bit odd to her the other day. "Don't forget that personal relationships are a vital part of our work," he'd reminded her. "It isn't all bookwork by any means, you know . . . it's very important to know how to handle our clients." Surely that had been a bit unnecessary, Marion thought. Wasn't that just what she was doing in the office every day—learning how to handle clients?

She didn't know that quite a number of Stanford & Earle's clients had complained that Miss Gray seemed unsympathetic.

One afternoon at the end of August, she arrived home to find Eva alone in the house. She was working night shift at the factory this month, and was eating "breakfast": scrambled dried-egg and bacon at five o'clock in the afternoon.

"You're early," Eva commented as she poured Marion a cup of tea.

Marion sat down at the kitchen table with its worn, shiny oilcloth cover.

"We're a bit slack at the office just now. We have been for some time, as a matter of fact. It's not surprising when you think about it—there're no new buildings going up, and people seem to prefer to stay put in wartime. Mr. Stanford says it'll be a different story as soon as the war ends; there won't be enough houses to go round, with all the men coming back. . . . Oh. Oh, I'm sorry, Evie, I didn't think."

For Eva had winced at her sister's tactlessness.

It was hot and stuffy in the little kitchen. But if you opened the window too wide, the smell from the gas-works pervaded the house. Marion fanned herself with the evening newspaper which she had bought on the way home. Eva screwed up her eyes to read the headlines.

"Duke—of—Kent—killed," she spelled out slowly. "Oh, how dreadful."

"Oh, yes," said Marion, "I meant to show you as soon as I got in. He crashed in a flying boat in the north of Scotland."

Eva's eyes darkened. Her thoughts went out to the young Duchess and her three children.

Marion's reaction to the news was more impersonal. The Duke of Kent was no more than a regal symbol to her, hardly to be thought of as a real person. This was the way she thought of all the Royal Family— though recent photographs showing the King and Queen and the two Princesses engaged in stirrup-pump drill in the grounds of Buckingham Palace had seemed to bring them nearer to "ordinary people."

She sighed, and looked round the kitchen with a dissatisfied expression. Her glance took in the old-fashioned cooking range which her mother still black-leaded every week, the low-slung china sink, the littered flypapers suspended from the ceiling light.

"I wish Mum and Dad would move from here," she said. "They'd find a nice new little house much easier to run—one of those bungalows on the Sandilands Estate, for instance. House prices have fallen so much—I wonder if Dad could afford to buy, if one came into the market. I expect we could arrange a mortgage . . ."

"Sandilands Estate! That was where Ken and I . . . We used to go up there sometimes, Sunday afternoons, and imagine we lived in one of those bungalows."

Eva vividly recalled those Sunday expeditions into the countryside around Renchester. The rows of red-brick bungalows with their variegated roofs stood on the edge of farming land, the farthest tentacles of Renchester's octopus growth. Their front doors had shone with glossy paint, and they were signposted with names like "Mon Repos," "Le Nid," "Green Verges," "Sunnyfield," done in wrought iron or poker-work.

Marion sighed again. It seemed impossible to say anything without reminding Eva of her precious Ken. It was selfish, really, the way she related everything to herself. She should think of other people for a change. After all, she was young—she'd probably marry again quite soon. And it would have been worse if she'd had a child to look after. Marion decided to tell her sister this.

"It's—it's awful about Ken," she began. "But at least you can be thankful there isn't a baby to cope with, and have to bring up on your own."

Then she stopped, frightened by the way Eva was staring at her.

"What's the matter with you, Marion?" Eva asked in a slow voice. "What makes you the way you are, so cold and mean? Do you know that you couldn't have said a more hurtful thing if you'd tried?" Her voice broke. "We hoped—Ken and I—there would be a baby. We weren't afraid of life or death. If—if only I had a baby, it would be something left of him, something warm and living. It's no good just remembering. I—can't—remember what he looked like properly. I—can't—even—remember his face!"

She was sobbing as she spoke. Marion, white-faced, put down her tea cup. Her hand shook. "I'm sorry I spoke," she said bitterly, and went upstairs to her room.

She stood by her bedroom window, looking out at the familiar, dreary prospect before her. Not for the first time, she thought she must leave home, find work somewhere else. London? It was a daring thought. Yet why not? Not yet—she'd wait until she had passed her exams and was fully qualified. There were sure to be openings in estate agents' offices in London. Suddenly she felt that the future was exciting, challenging. She heard the front door slam, and saw Eva going down the road. She watched her as she passed the advertisement for Mawton's Mineral Waters, peeling off the side-wall of the corner shop: a man and a girl in sports clothes, their lips forever at the rims of two glasses brimful of sparkling orangeade. Alongside it on the hoarding was one of the home-front propaganda posters—*Go Easy on Bread, Eat Potatoes Instead*. Then Eva turned the corner, going out of sight.

Marion's expression hardened. She'd show Eva—all of them—that she belonged to a bigger world than Povey Street!

The High School shelters had been constructed within the old cellars that ran beneath the building. Steel girders had been erected to strengthen the walls, and a new lighting system installed so that lessons interrupted by the siren's warning could be continued underground. Although there had been no air raids for months (the air offensive was now almost wholly British—each week, thousands of tons of bombs were being dropped on Germany's industrial centers), the headmistress still considered it a wise precaution to hold important examinations in the shelters so that the candidates could write their papers without interruption.

During the winter term of 1942, the Fifth Form sat for "mock matric." This was to prepare them for the real exam, which they would take next year. For one week in early December, they sat at folding desks in the shelters, reading the exam papers through carefully, exchanging silent grimaces of disgust or—occasionally— expressions of delight at what they saw; and industriously covering sheets of paper with their answers to the questions—or else chewing the end of a pen and sitting in hopeless inactivity. What a difference could lie between the two commands of the invigilator: "You may begin" and: "Stop writing now!"

Anna's dark head was bent happily over the language papers, Latin and French, but she did not enjoy the math and chemistry exams. Flora, on the other hand,

sighed over the Latin and French, but felt at ease with
the science papers.

She had decided she would like to be a physiotherapist
when she left school. It was funny, she reflected, when
Pauline had left school, only a little while ago really, no
one had suggested she should think of a career. But now
both the teaching staff and your parents seemed to take it
for granted that you should do a job. Flora was glad;
she thought it would be very dull just to stay at home
and do nothing in particular. Of course, if the war was
still on when she left, there would be no choice about it,
anyway—she'd be called up when she was eighteen. She
knew Pauline had found it boring in the end, just being
at home. Flora wondered why everyone thought differ-
ently about girls doing jobs now; it must be the general
atmosphere of wanting to help the war effort, and the
fact that women were doing men's work nowadays, she
supposed.

After each exam ended that week, there were eager
postmortems on the papers. "Well, what did you think
of it?"—"Did you see the catch in question 7?"—"Had
you revised Reproduction in the Rabbit?"—"I made it
come to 800 cubic feet."—"*Should* it have been subjunc-
tive? Oh, heavens!"

Anna did not discuss the exam papers so lightheartedly
as the other girls. To her, it was essential that she should
achieve credit marks all around, for she wanted to read
modern languages at the University; her only hope of
getting there was to do well in these important examinations, and then win a scholarship from the Sixth Form.
It was different for Flora, and for most of the other girls
—the carefree English Annes and Joans and Elizabeths.

But Anna Jelinck must always prove herself in her adopted country; prove that she was something more than "that foreign girl with the funny name."

On the Thursday after she had written all she could think of for the final question of the history exam ("Discuss the causes of the French Revolution"), Anna sat at her desk with her answers neatly arranged in front of her. Her thoughts wandered away from the examination room, the scratching pens, and rustle of paper. She thought of the sad little joke her father had made at supper last night. He had been to tune a piano at some music teacher's house, and had waited while a small boy who cared nothing for music had finished his lesson, scrambling through a version of "The Merry Peasant." "And then," her father had said, recounting the incident, suddenly I am remembering the time when first we are in England, and I am playing in the eating house. And I think—why, that is me, I am the Merry Peasant!—In the shiny silk blouse with such sleeves, they fall down to the violin when I play!"

Her poor father. He was so patient. Anna felt that any success of hers would, in a sense, compensate for his disappointments. The Merry Peasant! How Tomas would have smiled in disbelief that his father should ever describe himself so ironically. Her thoughts came back to her surroundings. Tomas had always been carefree enough about exams. "The important thing to remember about an examination," she remembered him saying once, with a solemn expression on his face, "is this: either you pass it or you fail it!" And he had burst into a roar of laughter, his black eyes crinkling.

"Thus it will be seen," Flora wrote with a flourish, "that there were many reasons why the Bourbons were finally deposed from power in France."

She blotted the last sentence carefully, then sat back and waited for the hands of the clock to come round to the half hour. She began to doodle idly on her square of pink blotting paper, then decided to rule a line at the end of her answer to the last question. Before the war, you used to have to write on one side of the paper only in exams, but now, because of the paper shortage, you used both sides and made sure your margins weren't too wide. She picked up her ruler—and then stayed unmoving in her chair, staring at the name faintly written along one side: JANET MURDOCH, Lwr IV.

Flora had lost her own ruler the day before, and had snatched this one from a drawer in the hall table before setting out for school that morning. Janet's ruler. They often used to do their homework together at Parklands, before . . . Janet must have left it behind one evening.

Flora remembered well the morning two years ago when their form-mistress in Lower IV had told them Janet had been killed in the air raid the previous night. Flora had scarcely been able to understand the news. Janet dead? It seemed illogical; why, less than twenty-four hours ago, she had been told off for giggling during a singing lesson. It had happened so suddenly. After that day, you simply didn't see Janet again. Other girls with whom Flora had been friendly had left school, moved away from the town—but you knew they were *there,* somewhere in the same world.

Flora glanced across at Anna, who had also finished writing, and was obviously lost in her own thoughts. Anna had been the last to see Janet; they had gone home together on the bus, as usual, and—"See you tomorrow!" Janet had called cheerfully as Anna got off at the stop before hers. Anna hadn't wanted to talk about Janet afterwards, Flora recalled. The three of them had been good friends: Flora herself felt that she wanted to remember all the things they used to do together. But then Anna hardly ever mentioned her brother, either— Tomas, who had disappeared one day, as suddenly as Janet. Flora suspected Anna thought about Tomas a good deal, though. Perhaps she even hoped he was still alive.

Janet had written her name in ink. Flora licked the end of her forefinger and slowly rubbed out the letters. Now it was just an ordinary varnished wooden ruler, the same as the one she had lost yesterday.

The hour hand of the clock hovered on half past twelve. In the dinner break, she and Anna planned to look at some copies of an American magazine called *Seventeen* that Andrew MacIntyre's mother had sent over with a food parcel. Flora's mother had been thrilled to receive tins of coffee, butter, and ham. "Bundles for Britain," parcels from America were called; they made the perilous crossing of the Atlantic in cargo ships escorted by convoys of the Royal Navy.

In the face of ceaseless U-boat attacks, the convoys somehow kept the Atlantic trade route open, so that much-needed supplies of food and arms could reach Britain. Hitler had not succeeded in his aim to blockade Britain and starve her into surrender, though at times— especially early that year—he had come very near to doing so.

Flora thought about Andy. It seemed pretty definite

that Pauline would marry him. She and Andy were much more *serious* together, somehow, than she and Clive had been. Flora liked Andy; he'd visited Parklands twice on brief leaves. The fact that he was an American didn't seem to matter, once you got used to his slight accent. When he first saw Parklands, he'd remarked that his parents' house was on a similar sort of estate in New England, only without so many walls and fences dividing neighboring gardens. But Flora recalled one difference that had stood out. They'd all been listening to one of Tommy Handley's ITMA programs. (In common with most families, the Stanfords were fans of this fast-moving weekly radio show and its quick comedian. The show's catch phrases—"Can I do you now, sir?"—"I don't mind if I do"—"After *you,* Claude: no, after *you,* Cecil"—had become common coin throughout Britain.) That particular evening, they had laughed aloud as usual at the ridiculous situations and the cheerful backchat. But Andy hadn't laughed. He'd sat looking rather embarrassed, as people do when they simply can't agree something is funny.

"I guess there's quite a difference in British and American humor," he'd said afterwards.

Both Andy and Pauline had leave soon after Christmas. Her mother was planning a party for them, saving precious rations to provide a buffet supper. It would be Flora's first grown-up party; she was to wear a renovated cocktail dress that had been Pauline's. The skirt was far too long—dresses had been down to the ankles in 1938. Now they were just below the knee. Clothes rationing had been in force for a year and a half now. The sixty-six coupons a year you were allowed meant that chances of getting new clothes were strictly limited. Most of the coupons went on school uniform, anyway, though the High School had relaxed many of the rules about that. A pair of shoes took as many as seven coupons, and stockings three. Flora was saving her one and only pair of silk stockings to wear at the party. In *Seventeen,* there were advertisements for some marvelous new stockings called nylons. Perhaps you would be able to buy nylons in England after the war. . . . Andy's mother had sent copies of *Seventeen* before, and Flora and Anna had sighed together over the gorgeous clothes that teenage American girls were wearing. Nowadays, everyone was busy remaking old clothes—and her mother had made herself a housecoat out of furnishing fabric, which took fewer coupons than dress materials. Even handkerchiefs were one coupon each. . . .

Flora's thoughts reverted to the French Revolution. Wasn't there a story about Marie Antoinette ordering all the courtiers at Versailles to use round handkerchiefs instead of square ones? Suddenly, she remembered something she had left out of her answer to that question. The Salt Tax! That had been one of the final straws that triggered off the Revolution. She reached for her pen.

But Miss Andrews, who was invigilating, looked over the top of her glasses. "Stop writing now."

Christmas, 1942, brought a surge of hope that the beginning of the end of the war was in sight. In October, Britain had launched a great new offensive in Egypt; after eleven days of fierce fighting, the Axis forces were in full and disordered retreat—it was the end of their campaign in the Western Desert. Tobruk, that white sepulcher by the blue sea, was recaptured again by the British on November 13. In French North Africa, the Allied forces entered Tunisia. Raoul Duchesne was among the men of the Free French Army who took part in this new offensive.

In Russia, the Red Army had fought desperately throughout the summer to repulse a new German offensive begun in May. The German forces advanced rapidly as far as the Volga; in September, the siege of Stalingrad began. Stalin welcomed the success of the Allied offensive in North Africa, declaring that it had turned the war in Europe radically in favor of the Allies and would relieve the pressure on Russia. The battle for Stalingrad continued for three months; then, on November 19, the heroic Red Army encircled the German forces in the area. By the end of January, those forces were "liquidated" —a word that was part of the wartime vocabulary, as terribly expressive as the phrase "mopping-up operations."

The situation in the Far East was still critical, with further Japanese successes, but in the Pacific area the Americans were beginning to gain ground.

Could it really be that the tide had turned? That was the hope reflected in every mind as a new year of war began.

A Sapphire and Diamonds

During the hunting season, the *Renchester Echo* carried a column headed "Field Jottings." On a day of glaring sunshine in April, far from the muddy fields and five-barred gates, the copses and hedges and ditches of the hunting country around her home town, Suzanne sat by a dusty white road in Spain, listening to the cicadas whirring in the thyme scrub that covered the hillside, and recalled to mind fragments from those jottings.

"We met at the Dog and Fox, Briardale. Hounds left covert with a purposeful air . . . they ran southeast over Cleve Hill, past Trimble's Barn and into Glossop Bottom . . . a fresh fox bolted and went down into Scardale Wood and from there hounds hunted on over Borden Golf Course and back to Crippen Wood, where they marked to ground."

But there was one particular phrase she was trying to remember. How did it go? Ah, yes—"unfortunately scent failed in the heavy rain"—or, more simply: "Hounds ran out of scent."

Suzanne had always felt vaguely relieved when she read that and knew that the fox had gone away.

Now she was the fox who had gone away, escaped from France across the Pyrenees. But she did not feel safe yet. General Franco's rule in Spain was a new dictatorship; his military police, the Guardia Civil, appeared to Suzanne as sinister figures in spite of the touch of comic opera supplied by their shiny black tricorns. Two stood guarding the approach to every village she passed through, two more the road that led away from the village. Wearing gray-green uniforms, bayonets fixed on their rifles, they stood opposite each other in the shade of the wayside olive trees with their gray-green foliage. Suzanne was careful to avoid their scrutiny. She made detours into the surrounding countryside, coming down into the villages by way of the hill paths. She did not want to be hauled into a primitive guardroom for interrogation, and subsequently, perhaps, thrown into a small Spanish jail for an indefinite period.

She would not feel secure until she reached Barcelona and contacted the British Consul. He would hear her story and arrange a passage back to England. When she arrived home, Suzanne knew she would have to go through her experiences step by step with senior MI5 officers. Her smallest observation might contain important information. Her training had served her well during her flight along the escape route; she had noticed what military vehicles were traveling the roads, which enemy troops crowded the railway termini, the location of certain airfields . . .

She got up and began walking again. Her feet had hardened now; she no longer winced with the pain of ill-fitting shoes. As she went along the narrow road that snaked its way alongside the rocky Spanish coatline, her escape arranged itself in her mind as a pattern of shoes.

First, there were the carefully chosen black walking shoes she had worn when first she arrived in France. They had worn out after a twenty-mile hike made under cover of darkness. Then Madame Lafitte, a gallant old lady who sheltered agents and escaped airmen in her house at Tours, had given Suzanne a pair of her own shoes. They were too long and too narrow—but they provided a layer of leather between the ground and the soles of her feet. Madame Lafitte's winkle-pickers had lasted through the winter, during the cold, wet tramps through town streets. Louis, the guide who finally led her across the yellow route into Spain (only that was not his real name, of course), had found her a pair of small-size French army boots for the trek over the mountains. These Suzanne had thankfully abandoned as soon as she reached the first village with a general store. The Resistance organization had provided her with a small amount of pesetas to pay for food and shelter, and she bought a pair of blue espadrilles from a bunch of rope-soled sandals hanging outside the doorway of the shop.

That was a week ago. Now Suzanne was very near where she planned to take a train to Barcelona. Her other clothes were in poor shape, too; Madame Lafitte had given her a black jersey that smelled of mothballs, to replace the thin silk blouse she had set out in from England. Her light-colored raincoat was stained and torn, her stockings had been discarded long ago. Her skin was

deeply tanned from exposure to rain and wind and sun,
and she had lost weight during her trek. She looked like a
Romany girl.

When at last she boarded the train for Barcelona and
settled down in a second-class compartment with plain
wooden seats, she could scarcely believe she was really
on the last lap of her journey to safety. She felt, at this
moment, that she had had enough of high adventure to
last her lifetime. She knew that the recounting of her
experiences afterwards was bound to seem exciting, even
fascinating; described however flatly, they would take on
a sort of glamour. They were the stuff out of which spy
films were made. Only, she thought ruefully as she
folded her dirty raincoat and laid it on the seat beside
her, the heroine's make-up would remain unimpaired to
the bitter end!

And in a film, only the exciting moments would be
shown, the moments of acute tension and most significant
action. There would be a shot of her final encounter with
the street artist in Paris, for example, but no glimpses of
the tedious hours spent *waiting* . . . sitting in seedy
cafés, drinking cup after cup of ersatz coffee, *waiting*
for a contact to announce himself; hanging about railway
stations, *waiting* for some one else to press a train ticket
into her hand; shut in a stuffy room with one indifferent,
yellowed novel for occupation, *waiting* for the news that
Louis was ready to conduct her over the mountains. . . .
How infinitely preferable to lead an ordinary life! To
visit cafés simply to meet a friend or quench your thirst;
to tender your railway fare in a ticket office in the normal
way; to be able to walk out of rooms you didn't enjoy
sitting in, out into the sunshine!

The refrain of a comic song that had been in the air about the time she joined the staff at Renchester High School fell into her thoughts:

Olga Pulloffski, the beautiful spy!
The gay Continental rapscallion.
Some say she's Russian, and some say she's French,
But her accent is Gin and Italian . . .

Well, that was one way of looking at a woman agent, Suzanne supposed: "the brunette with eyes black as jet" who, waltzing around with the General, "robs the old sport of the plans of the fort"—and "sells them for ten million sterling." Certainly there had been plenty of Olga Pulloffskis in the past. As the train rattled on towards Barcelona, Suzanne amused herself by recalling some of the more infamous. There was Delilah, of course . . . and Mata Hari! She'd once read a potted account of Mata Hari's life—she was a Dutch girl, a night-club dancer, who spied for both the Germans and the French in turn during the 1914 war, and was finally shot for her treachery by the French.

Suzanne stared out of the carriage window. Mata Hari had met death bravely, she remembered, refusing to let them bandage her eyes. . . .

As the train approached the outskirts of Barcelona, her thoughts returned to Paris and to the woman who was known as "the Cat." Micheline Carré had belonged to a Resistance cell called l'Interallié. Like Suzanne, she had been a schoolteacher. In 1940, she'd set up a radio transmitter in a house close by the Arc de Triomphe, under the noses of the Germans. Almost nightly, London received her messages: *To Room 55a, War Office. The Cat reports.* At the end of 1941, the Gestapo had arrested the Cat. She expected to be shot: instead, a clever German officer had visited her in prison and persuaded her to act as a German agent. The Cat continued to send messages to London—messages supplied by the Germans. She helped the three German battleships *Scharnhorst, Gneisenau,* and *Prinz Eugen* to escape from France to Germany by leading British Intelligence to believe the ships were lying crippled in Brest harbor. After this, London no longer trusted the Cat, and she became useless to the Germans. Believing that the Gestapo were about to arrest her a second time, she fled to London. Only a little while before, she would have been welcomed as a heroine of the French Resistance . . . now, she was denounced by other Resistance fighters in England who knew that she had been arrested by the Gestapo weeks before the three German battleships escaped through the Channel.

Suzanne had heard Micheline Carré's story from Marcel, the pastry cook who had sheltered her in his attic room in Paris.

The train slowed down and drew alongside a platform in a busy station. Barcelona! Suzanne stepped down from the carriage. It seemed curious to be among a crowd of people who were at peace. Yet only a short time ago, these Catalonians had been fighting their own war; the country was exhausted by civil strife. There was evidence of this everywhere. No one gave the girl in the grubby white mackintosh and blue espadrilles a second glance; there were plenty of others dressed in rags, existing in extreme poverty.

Suzanne knew where the British Consulate was situated, and set off briskly. The hot sun struck with the force almost of a physical blow as she left the shade of the station arcades and crossed a wide plaza. She hurried along a street flanked by trees planted at intervals, welcoming the patches of shade thrown down by their foliage. (Once Gavin Cortley had dodged from doorway to doorway along this same street, avoiding snipers' bullets.) Tonight, thought Suzanne, she would wear clean clothes, sleep in a comfortable bed, and know the benison of hot water once again!

Lily Mawton came into the morning room at Briardale and settled herself in her favorite armchair to read the newspaper. They hardly ever sat in the drawing room now. It was difficult to spare the fuel to warm it. They had reverted to the custom of every Renchester back street, Lily thought with a smile: keep the parlor for company.

She scanned the front-page news. How quiet it was without the children! When it seemed certain that the Germans had given up their bombing offensive, the evacuees had gone home again, many of them looking more healthy and fit than they had ever done before. Some of them still came out to Briardale at weekends, for Lily had won a place in their affections as a deputy mother. She missed the noise of their feet clattering about the house, the sound of their shrill voices in the grounds, and the welcome responsibility of all those plates to fill around the big kitchen table.

Her attention was wandering from the news. The headlines concerned the end of the war in North Africa. A

fortnight ago, following the final great offensive of the
Allied armies in Tunisia, all organized resistance by Axis
troops in North Africa had come to an end. General von
Arnim, who had succeeded Rommel as Commander-in-
Chief of the German forces, had been captured, along
with seventeen other enemy generals.

Spectacular successes crowned that month of May: the
RAF had recently struck their most devastating blow of
the war by smashing the walls of the Mohne and Eder
dams, causing huge floods to sweep through the Ruhr
Valley. Today, there was news of further RAF attacks on
Essen and Dortmund.

Lily read of more advances by the Americans against
the Japanese in the Pacific area; then she turned to the
Court page. She liked to read the announcements of forthcoming marriages; sometimes there was a Rencastrian
name she knew. A short while ago, for instance, the engagement of Esmé Beaton and Gordon Pearce had been
announced. When she head that, Lily's thoughts had
gone back to the Briardale housewarming party. Esmé's
mother had worn a silver lamé dress that everyone had
considered very daring . . . young Dr. Pearce had come to
the party with Dr. Sinclair and his daughter—and there
had been rather a heated discussion in the drawing room.
How long ago it all seemed!

She glanced down the column. So many names, both
men and women, were prefixed by their service rank.
Then, halfway down, she saw this:

Capt. A. I. MacIntyre and
L/Wren P. M. Stanford

The engagement is announced between Capt. Andrew Ian MacIntyre, only son of Mr. and Mrs. W. A. MacIntyre, of Landfall Point, Massachusetts, U.S.A., and Pauline Mary, elder daughter of Mr. and Mrs. J. R. Stanford, of 7 Parklands, Renchester.

Pauline Stanford engaged! Lily laid down the newspaper on her lap. To an American! She felt disappointed. She'd realized, of course, that Clive and Pauline weren't seeing so much of each other nowadays, but she'd hoped it was only a temporary cooling-off. . . . What a pity! Lily liked Pauline; she would have made an ideal wife for Clive. Much better than this Valerie that Clive seemed to be taken up with at the moment. She was a WAAF he'd met at a dance. He'd brought her down to Briardale once—a feather-brained little thing, a Londoner, with a Veronica-Lake lock of hair hanging over one eye. Lily had been making chutney the day they arrived, using windfalls from the apple orchard. Valerie's eyes had widened when she saw the array of glass jars.

"It's much easier to buy it in a shop!" she'd giggled.

The morning-room door opened, and Henry came in. Lily showed him the announcement of Pauline's engagement, and told him her thoughts about it.

"I'd far rather have had Pauline for a daughter-in-law than that Valerie," she said.

Henry Mawton was inclined to champion Valerie; she had seemed very feminine to him, with her appealing ways and petite figure. "Valerie's all right, a nice little girl," he said now. "The Stanfords were always a bit standoffish, you know. John Stanford thought his daughter was too good for Clive—never said so, of course, but I could tell."

Lily bridled at this. "I don't know why he should think

that, I'm sure. We're as good as they are, any day. Oh,
I know John Stanford went to public school—but so did
our Clive."

Henry Mawton shrugged. "I'm not ashamed of the fact
that I've made my own way in life." He paused. "I
shouldn't wonder if John Stanford isn't feeling the draft
a bit at the moment. Not much money to be made in
property nowdays." He puffed at his pipe, secure in the
knowledge that munitions were swelling his own finances
as much as mineral waters had ever done. He'd made a
joke on those lines at the Rotary Club the other day—
"High explosives of one sort or another have always been
my line." They'd had a good laugh at that one.

"He'll soon pick up again come the peace," Lily replied.
"It's always the same after a war; not enough houses to
go round. He'll even sell our old house in Parklands—
you'll see!"

"That'll be the day." Her husband pushed tobacco into
the bowl of his pipe with one thumb. "I was up there the
other morning . . . they've planted potatoes in the lawn!"
He sighed heavily, thinking of the smooth green turf
that had been his pride and joy. When the bombing was
at its height, 4 Parklands had been requisitioned by the
Council for two bombed-out families from downtown.

"More bombing of Germany," Lily remarked, indicating the newspaper on her knee. "They are getting a pasting and no mistake."

"They gave us a pasting and all," her husband retorted.
"Well, we've certainly paid 'em back in their own coin.
There can't be much of Berlin left now. Nine hundred
tons of bombs we dropped there during that raid in

March, double what they gave us in the worst raid of the blitz."

Lily shook her head. "It's a terrible war." She got out of her chair and crossed to her writing desk by the window. "I must write to Clive and tell him about Pauline. He never reads the newspaper properly; like as not he won't have seen the announcement."

Henry Mawton stood for a moment, gazing out of the window. He noticed some weeds in the stone urns along the terrace. He'd have to get down to those at the weekend. . . .

"Eh, Lily, you and I rattling about in this great house!" he remarked suddenly. "I reckon Lady Cortley did a sensible thing when she moved into her cottage."

Lily, filling her fountain pen, raised her eyebrows. Surely Harry wasn't thinking of forsaking Briardale House, his realized ambition? His next words reassured her.

"Still," he said, "it'll be different after the war—when we get a staff back, and have our grandchildren running about the house."

"Don't tempt Providence, Harry," Lily said quite sharply. "We've a long way to go yet. Please God, Clive will be spared. He can marry Valerie, or any other girl he likes, just so long as he comes through all right."

Her husband grunted, picked up the newspaper, and settled himself in the armchair. There was quiet, broken only by the sound of a pen nib on paper, the occasional turning of newspaper pages, and the drawing of his pipe.

Suzanne peered out of the plane window, watching the

blue coastline recede into the distance. They were out of their element now, she and her fellow passengers—amid a world of cloud above and sea below. She was lucky to have got a place so soon on one of the few civilian flights between Lisbon and London.

After a short stay in Barcelona, she had been sent on to Lisbon for "screening" by British Intelligence. There were many enemy agents who tried to enter England with bogus stories that they had escaped from occupied territory to fight for the Allies, or were Resistance fighters or even British agents on the run from the Gestapo. Suzanne had proved herself satisfactorily, and earned official commendation for her successful escape from a tricky situation. She learned, too, that when she failed to return at the appointed time, another agent was sent to France, and had successfully delivered the message with which she had been entrusted. And now she was en route for home. In a few hours they would land in London.

She glanced around at the other people on the plane. Then she looked again at the slim, fair-haired man with the handsome profile who was sitting with a book unopened on his knee. Surely that was Leslie Howard, the actor! Yes, she was certain of it. Suzanne smiled, remembering the time when she'd confiscated a photograph of him that was being passed round the form-room during a French lesson. He must be returning home from ENSA work with the troops. She recalled his performance as Professor Higgins in the film of "Pygmalion." Pygmalion! Suzanne settled back in her seat. She was a sort of Galatea herself, schoolteacher turned spy. It would look well as the title of a serial in the *News of the World*!

She studied the famous actor again. She'd last seen him in "Gone With the Wind." She'd even persuaded her father to see that epic, though as a rule he never went to a cinema. "Quite splendid, my dear," he'd said afterwards. "I really enjoyed it. So much larger than life."

Her father. . . . Suzanne planned to telephone him from London. How surprised he would be to hear her voice! How glad she would be to hear his. Then she would take the first possible train to Renchester. What was it those Government notices said above all the ticket offices in British stations—*Is Your Journey Really Necessary?* That was to keep the trains as free as possible for troop movements. Well, *her* journey certainly would be necessary, no doubt about that! A quiet few days of leave . . . bliss!

Perhaps she ought to phone Gordon, too, while she was in London. He might be hurt if she didn't. She guessed that he would have been in contact with her father during her protracted absence, and of course her father would have been officially told she was engaged on a Special Mission. . . . Thinking of Gordon, Suzanne sighed. If only he would find someone else to marry!

Did they still go through the prewar customs ritual now, she wondered! Have you anything to declare? She'd bought a bottle of scent and some silk stockings in Lisbon. One of the British Embassy staff, who'd taken her out one evening for her first good meal for several months, had advised her to buy the scent. "There's a hundred per cent tax on luxury goods at home since the last budget," he'd told her. That made Chanel No. 5 a bit expensive. . . .

The plane gave a lurch, then heeled sideways, staggering. Everyone was suddenly alert; luggage tumbled from the overhead racks. Then, insidiously, the smell of burning grew. . . .

Suzanne gripped the back of the seat in front of her and began to fumble with her parachute harness. While she had been indulging herself in rambling thoughts, lulled into a false sense of security, some danger had ambushed them from the clouds. . . . She was thrown violently forward as the plane pitched into a steep, spinning dive.

In London, the air was mild for early June; office girls hurrying back from their lunch hour wore cotton frocks, and there were straw hats displayed in the milliners' shop windows. Bond Street still managed to impart an impression of exclusive luxury in spite of bomb damage and the 100 per cent purchase tax. The doorway of the jeweler's shop was sandbagged for safety. The sandbags had been there since 1940; some of them had split, and spilled their gold dust over the pavement.

"It's heavenly, darling, absolutely perfect. Bless you!" Esmé traced the outline of the sapphire and diamond ring inside her glove.

Gordon pressed her arm and smiled down at her. "Only what you deserve, my love."

Seeing them, passers-by smiled involuntarily; Esmé's ring might just as well have been sewn on her sleeve. They waited to cross the road. A Rolls glided down to Piccadilly, conveying some VIP. An official flag waved on the bonnet.

"When you're a famous surgeon, darling, you shall

have a much slinkier Rolls-Royce than that, with a built-in stethoscope," Esmé said.

"Too difficult to park in Harley Street," Gordon replied. "Buy me an Austin Seven instead."

"Oh, look——" Esmé stopped on a corner where a newspaper placard was displayed:

PLANE OVERDUE: FAMOUS FILM STAR
VANISHES

"I must know who it is. Have you a penny?"

"What, a penny as well as a diamond and all those sapphires?" Gordon fished in his trouser pocket for the coin.

He looked over Esmé's shoulder while she read the front-page story.

"Oh." Suddenly her voice lost its gaiety. "It's Leslie Howard. He was on a plane coming from Lisbon. It's believed to have crashed. Apparently there's no hope of picking up any survivors—it doesn't mention anyone else on the plane; he must have been the only well-known passenger."

"I wonder if it was attacked by an enemy raider," Gordon said.

"Apparently it was a civilian flight," Esmé said. "Not that that means anything." Her voice grew hard. "Nothing is immune, is it? Not gentle-mannered actors, nor hospitals, nor schools." She thought of the recent daylight raid on London during which a school was singled out as a target by a low-flying German bomber, and forty-five children had been killed.

"Nothing, no one," Gordon answered.

They walked on in silence. It seemed chilly now;

there wasn't much warmth in the early summer sushine,
after all. They hurried through to Regent Street. Gordon
was on duty that afternoon; their visit to buy the engagement ring had been snatched out of a busy day. Esmé was
going to buy sheets and pillowcases at a Regent Street
store, with precious coupons donated by fond aunts—for
household linen too was rationed. She and Gordon parted
outside the shop, happy in the knowledge that they
would see each other again that evening.

It was June—June, the bridal month, and there were
white wedding gowns displayed in the shop window.
Esmé went through the swing door into the warm interior of the store, excited as any girl buying linen for her
bottom drawer. Just inside the door, a branched stand
was cunningly draped with a collection of fine woollen
head scarves in jewellike colors. Her attention was caught
by them, as it was meant to be. But scarves were three
coupons. . . . Then she thought of Lorna, who never ventured outside without the inevitable head scarf tied under
her chin.

Impulsively, Esmé proffered money and her pink cloth-
ing-coupon book over the counter. Snip, snip—bang went
three coupons that would have purchased a pair of pillow-
slips. But the gay scarf was a cheerful thought, and she
was probably the only person who guessed just how much
Lorna needed cheering at the moment. Esmé knew that
Andy MacIntyre's engagement to Pauline Stanford had
been a real blow. "No more than you deserve," Gordon
had said about her gorgeous new ring; well, Lorna certainly deserved that scarf. "As a small token of my appre-
ciation!" Esmé said to herself, in the tone of voice she

and Lorna used to use together. They'd been good friends. . . .

Somewhere on the route from Lisbon to London, a plane had vanished. No one ever discovered exactly what had happened; and the clouds and the cold sea kept their counsel.

Before the Leaves
of Autumn Fall

Empty your pockets, Tom, Dick and Harry,
Strip your identity; leave it behind . . .

Tom, Dick and Harry, plain names and numbers,
Pilot, observer, and gunner depart.
Their personal litter only encumbers
Somebody's head, somebody's heart.

The words of the poem ran through Clive Mawton's
mind as he prepared to leave base for a reconnaissance
flight. Poetry—the old Shelley and Keats routine—wasn't
much in Clive's line as a rule, but these particular verses
had stuck in his head, maybe because they described a
security precaution he himself carried out almost daily.
(Who ever stopped to listen to a nightingale in this day
and age?)

more! Some of the chaps talked of staying with planes; there'd surely be scope for civil airline pilots—and of course there was always the plum, the test pilot's job. But cars were Clive's first love. That was a nice little Lagonda he'd had in '38 . . .

A buzz of talk came from the Ops. Room. A hearty voice told Clive to snap out of it and come down to earth. Clive grinned, shook off his thoughts, and joined in the cheerful badinage around him. This was the life!

At the end of June, 1943, Winston Churchill warned the Axis that there would be heavy fighting in the Mediterranean and elsewhere "before the leaves of autumn fall." The following month, British, American, and Canadian troops invaded Sicily, capturing twelve towns in two days, including the port of Syracuse. And on July 25, Benito Mussolini resigned his dictatorship. The Fascist regime in Italy was ended after twenty-one years. King Victor Emmanuel, who had remained a figurehead during Mussolini's reign, now assumed command of the Italian forces. The invasion of Sicily was completed in mid-August. American and Canadian forces occupied Lipari and Stromboli—that glowing volcanic island that used to be the nightly cynosure of tourists' eyes during prewar Mediterranean pleasure cruises.

On September 3, the fifth anniversary of the outbreak of war, the Allies invaded the Toe of Italy, and soon held forty miles of the Calabrian coast. On September 8, General Dwight Eisenhower, formerly in command of North Africa, and now Allied commander in chief of the Second Front in Europe, announced the unconditional surrender of Italy. But the battle within Italy continued as the Brit-

Name, rank, and number . . . that was all you divu
if you crashed and were captured by the enemy. N
rank, and number . . .

Clive laid out the contents of his pockets on top o
tallboy. If he didn't come back, they would be hand
over to his C.O., who would post them to his next of l
—his mother—with the usual letter of sympathy. ("Cl
was a lively member of the squadron; he will be deep
missed by all his colleagues . . .") There wasn't much:
photograph of Val, smiling so that her nose tip-tilte
rather sweetly; a gold watch that had belonged to h
grandfather, with his initials and a date: HVM, 1872. A
bill from his tailor. And his mother's latest letter, with
the news of Pauline's engagement.

Clive fastened his flying jacket, whistling noncha-
lantly. Good old Pauline, marrying a Yankee! He'd written her a letter, hoping she'd be happy and all that. Dear
Mother, she'd been frightfully tactful when she broke the
news; perhaps she imagined it would be a bitter blow to
him. If so, she couldn't be more wrong. There was no
question of his marrying anyone at the moment, so far
as he was concerned. After the war . . . well, Val was a
good sport, and more fun than Pauline had ever been.
Perhaps they'd end up as man and wife. Who could tell?

He picked up his gloves and sauntered off to the Ops.
Room for the briefing. Outside, on the airfield, the planes
waited for take-off like dogs anticipating the promise of
a run.

After it was all over, Clive mused as he walked on, he
might work with cars; perhaps he'd open a garage or
two. Renchester could do with a really first-class garage.
No stooging around his father's factory for him any

ish Fifth Army entered Naples and pursued the fleeing German troops to the Volturno River. Italy now declared war on Germany in face of her "repeated and intensified acts of war committed against Italians," and was accepted as a co-belligerent by the Allies.

The Allied advance against the Germans continued through the winter; in January, 1944, there was bitter fighting on the Anzio beachhead, south of Rome. The bombing of the Monte Cassino Abbey destroyed the strongest German defense on the road to Rome; it seemed only a matter of time before the victorious Allies would enter the capital of Italy.

"Germany is standing on the edge of catastrophe," Stalin told the world after the capitulation of Italy. His Red Army went from strength to strength, driving the Nazi forces out of Russia. In January, the Russians entered Poland; by April, they had invaded Rumania and reached the frontier of Czechoslovakia.

At the other side of the world, the Japanese suffered heavy losses from the Americans. British troops in Burma made a firm stand to check a Japanese invasion of India. But on the last day of March, the British learned of a grievous loss in the death of Major-General Orde Wingate, leader and hero of the jungle war in Burma.

In England that spring of 1944, there was once again the anticipation of invasion. Four years ago, the anticipation had been fearful; now a gathering excitement was felt. It could not be long before the Allies launched a new and greater offensive in Europe, to drive the Germans out of France, out of Belgium, Holland, Denmark, Norway, and all the other occupied countries, back to Germany itself.

To prepare the ground for the impending invasion, the RAF's cross-Channel raids reached a new pitch of intensity. The aim was to disrupt all communication lines in France, and so hinder the Germans as much as possible in their defense and retreat. In April, a nonstop air attack lasting seven days reduced the French railway system and airfields to chaos. American airmen destroyed vital bridges in daring low-level attacks: there was hardly a bridge left in northern France strong enough to carry a panzer division.

Winston Churchill spoke to the nation: "The hour of our greatest effort and action is approaching."

These were days when, throughout Britain, every shadow-commander in chief of the Allied forces—every retired army officer, every pub politician—speculated where the invasion would actually begin, and how the forces would be deployed. Mustard pots and pepper mills, tankards and glasses, were moved from one strategic position to another as the possibilities were debated over dinner tables and at bar counters.

Southern England became an area shut off from the rest of the country so that the invasion preparations should be kept as secret as possible. Daily, the men and the materials of invasion—an endless stream of tanks, guns, trucks, armed bulldozers—poured down to the south coast. To mislead the enemy, mock preparations were made for a landing near Calais: dummy ships and tanks and sham airplanes were put on show near Dover. The Nazis, deceived by this ruse, moved troops to guard the Channel ports of France.

One morning, a Government appeal was broadcast over

the radio for photographs and home movie films taken
on the French coast in prewar days, which might now be
used in the detailed planning of the invasion.

Julia Cortley, breakfasting in the bright little kitchen
of Bay Tree Cottage, was among those who heard the
appeal. The announcer's voice was reduced to a whisper
over the old portable radio that she kept on the kitchen
dresser. The spare parts needed to rejuvenate it were
almost unobtainable now.

She stirred her coffee slowly; her mind's eye dipped
into the old photograph albums of prewar holidays spent
abroad. Italy had been the country the Cortleys visited
most: Venice, Naples, Rome. . . . Random memories
jogged her mind. Venice: the music of a military band
in the Piazza San Marco; the hot white dust in the
ruined streets of Pompeii, outside Naples; the musty smell
of an old-fashioned *carrozza,* touring the sights of Rome.
Venice, Naples, Rome. . . . Not even Venice had been
spared from air attack; the fleeing Germans had looted
Naples; there had been a ridiculous Allied air raid on
Pompeii, already so effectively destroyed by the eruption
of Vesuvius some two thousand years ago; Rome itself
would soon become a battleground.

But France—when had they ever visited France? Paris,
of course: the tourist's Paris of the Moulin Rouge, shopping in the Rue de Rivoli, the guided tour of Versailles.
But the French coast? Then she recalled three weeks one
August, spent on the coast of Brittany. A family holiday:
she and Hugo and Gavin. Sun-bathing on the sandy
beach . . . Hugo reading, in one of those hooded wicker-
work beach shelters . . . Gavin, at thirteen, swimming so

far out to sea that Julia had watched him anxiously, shad-
ing her eyes with one hand. "Don't worry about the boy,"
Hugo had said. "He'll be all right."

Of course: Hugo had been camera-mad that holiday!
He'd bought a Pathé ciné-camera at Wallace Heaton.
They'd filmed all sorts of things: a sequence on the
beach; the village church (the camera lens swooping up
to the spire and down again in true amateur fashion);
the peasants in their regional costume; the boats riding at
anchor in the harbor.

Could that old film serve a purpose now? She didn't
really think so. All the same, she decided to look at it
during the morning. The Government appeal gave her a
good excuse to indulge in some nostalgic memories. Mildred Lyall was arriving in the afternoon, coming to stay
for a few days. The old hand-projector Hugo had bought
to show his home movies was stored in the garage; she
and Mildred could run the film through that evening. . . .

"Strange how it always *rains* so heavily in these old
films," commented Mildred, sitting back in an armchair
as the prewar holiday reel unwound and cast its memories
on a white-distempered wall of the sitting room.

Julia had forgotten that rain effect, the flickering lines
over the pictures that made it seem as though you were
looking through a curtain of water.

"It will be better when I get the projector running
more smoothly," she said hopefully.

There it was, the dimly remembered beach, the sand
and the sea, and Julia herself in a strangely old-fashioned
bathing dress, smiling self-consciously from under the
brim of a wide white hat. There were those dear ghosts

(she had steeled herself throughout the day for this moment, half-longing for it, half-dreading it): Hugo, walking jerkily towards the camera, telling her to keep it steady as she took the picture; Gavin coming out of the sea, shaking the water from his hair. . . . Now they were in a boat, sailing into the harbor. The breeze, the breeze of yesterday, ruffled their clothes and whipped the sea into little waves. And here was the village church: Julia again, wearing an ankle-length cotton dress, with Gavin standing to attention by her side. Hugo had constantly complained they were too static. *"Move*—that's what it's for!" he'd admonished them, waving the camera about. Now for the swoop up to the church spire, hovering on the clock face an instant before coming down to earth again. A quarter past four in Brittany, 1933, when her life was not lived half in the shadows, as it was today. . . . That was the end of the reel. Nothing in it, Julia was sure now, that could help to plot the lie of the land for the invading troops.

Both women were silent as she rewound the film and put away the projector.

"Why should it be so much more poignant than looking at still snapshots?" Julia wondered aloud, offering Mildred cigarettes.

"Action is so—alive," Mildred replied. "At least we didn't hear their voices. That would be—unbearable."

Julia nodded. "One of Leslie Howard's films came to the local cinema last week. People watching the screen were crying, people who had never seen him in the flesh." She smiled gently. "I saw my daily help there, old Annie Whitelaw. The tears were trickling down her cheeks."

Mildred seized the opportunity to change the subject. She had feared it would be a mistake to revive those memories of Hugo and Gavin.

"You're very comfortable here," she remarked, looking round the sitting room. "What a blessing you moved when you did. Keeping up Briardale House must be a superhuman feat in wartime, even if you have plenty of money, as the Mawsons have."

"Mawtons," Julia corrected her. "Mawton's Mineral Waters. . . . Mrs. Mawton is so kind, she always presents me with jars of homemade crabapple jelly."

"I don't imagine domestic help will be any easier to find after the war's over," Mildred went on. "I can't see all those girls who've been earning good wages in factories suddenly turning round to become parlormaids and cooks as their mothers were before them."

Julia Cortley shrugged. "I suppose we've seen another of those English social revolutions the historians are so fond of enumerating," she said. "They will call them *bloodless*—I never understand why. Think of all those poor children who died as factory fodder in the Industrial Revolution . . . and *this* one has evolved out of four years of bloodshed to date."

"Tell me," Mildred said, with her usual habit of twisting lines of conversations to suit her own train of thought, "what's become of that Czech family the Central Refugee Committee settled in Renchester?"

"The Jelincks? They've become fairly—assimilated. I believe that's the word. That's to say, Josef Jelinck is now established as the most reliable piano tuner in town, and Anna, the daughter, is in the running for a University scholarship at the High School. I visit them occasionally when I go to Renchester."

"And the mother?"

"She's the least assimilated of all. She cooks with garlic and strange spices—*most* un-Rencastrian, and she still speaks English largely in the present tense or the infinitive."

"I don't imagine they'll ever return to their own country," Mildred said. "I wonder what conditions are like now that the Russians have taken over?"

"They won't go back if they're wise," Julia Cortley replied. "Russia was the hero of the day at the time of Stalingrad—but already it's becoming a very different story. Stalin is dedicated to the cause of Communism—he's not going to help us build a democratic peace after the war is over. After all, Russia is only our ally by force of circumstance, because Hitler invaded her."

Mildred glanced at the clock. "Good heavens," she exclaimed, "we almost missed Tommy Handley."

Julia switched on the sitting-room radio, then said: "If you don't mind, I'll leave you to listen alone. Somehow I don't feel in the mood for nonstop fun tonight. I think I'll read for a while in bed."

She left Mildred listening to the program, and went upstairs to finish a novel. But her innermost thoughts were still fixed on a summer day eleven years ago, and a boy who ran out from the sea.

Tuesday, June 6, 1944. "This is D-Day," came the announcement over the British radio, broadcasting to the peoples of Occupied Europe. "This is *the* day . . ." What hopes, what prayers were aroused in the hearts and minds of those who listened! Now, after the despairing years of enemy occupation, they received the blessed assurance that friends were approaching. . . .

The first waves of the Allied Invasion Army, commanded by General Bernard Montgomery, pressed inland from the beaches of Normandy, where floating Mulberry harbors had been built overnight. A long, flexible pipeline, known as "Pluto," ran beneath the sea from England to Normandy; thousands of gallons of fuel were pumped through it to keep the invasion armies mobile. Ten thousand airborne troops made massed landings behind the enemy lines.

There were heavy casualties as the German guns swept the beaches, but by June 7, the beachheads were cleared, and the beach forces made contact with their airborne units.

Back in England, King George VI visited Fort Southwick, Portsmouth, to watch work in progress on the Plot —a huge map marked with hundreds of movable symbols and manned by continuous shifts of workers, which followed the events of the invasion. The King came through one of the teleprinter rooms, where Pauline and other Wrens were busy sending out signals. They had all been instructed to make themselves extra smart that day, in honor of the quiet, diffident man who had come to see for himself how it fared with the invading armies.

By June 11, the Allied Front in Normandy was fifty-one miles wide and fifteen miles deep. The advance continued, with fierce opposition from the retreating Germans. The worst June storm for forty years broke over the beachhead and lasted three days. At the end of the month, there was a desperate tank battle in which the

Germans' crack panzer divisions were engaged. Early in July, Caen was captured. Then, on July 18, the great battle for France really began.

British and Canadian troops crossed the River Orme and broke through the German front. The Americans captured St. Lo. Germany's army in western Normandy was crippled; the Allies went on into Brittany. In August, landings were made in the south of France, and within a few days, a hundred miles of coastline between Nice and Marseilles lay in Allied hands.

Meanwhile, there was dramatic news from Prussia. Erich Hoffman, working amid a turmoil of files and papers in his office in Paris (all secret dossiers and important records were being sent into Germany for safety), learned with incredulity that an attempt had been made to assassinate the *Führer*.

"They tried—to kill the *Führer?*" He stared unbelievingly at his commandant, who had burst into his office with the news.

"It was an Army plot." The Commandant spat out the words; there was bitter rivalry between the Gestapo and the Army, particularly the Officer Korps.

"What happened?"

"The *Führer* was at the conference table. Colonel von Stauffenburg——"

"Von Stauffenburg!" Erich exclaimed. "He was decorated for service in North Africa——"

"Colonel von Stauffenburg," continued the Commandant, frowning at the interruption, "placed a briefcase containing a time bomb against a leg of the conference table, beside the *Führer's* chair." He paused dramatically.

"The bomb went off exactly as planned. Officers all around the table were killed. But the *Führer* escaped—by a miracle."

"A miracle!" Erich echoed.

"Actually, he was saved by the heavy table top, and the fact that the walls of the conference room collapsed, so lessening the blast of the explosion," the Commandant explained precisely.

His junior officer dismissed this scientific theory. "None the less, a miracle," he repeated.

The Commandant inclined his head.

"Have they arrested those responsible?"

"Hundreds of Army officers have been arrested and shot. My report states there have been over one thousand arrests: that may be an exaggeration." The Commandant paused. "Rommel was among those who instigated the plot. When he learned of its failure, he committed suicide."

Erich paled. "Rommel!"

The Commandant smiled contemptuously. "Officially it will be stated that he died of wounds received during the Allied attempt at invasion. The Officer Korps have never been truly loyal to the *Führer*." He drew himself up proudly. "Not as you and I are loyal to him. They accepted him as leader because there was no other choice. Now they pretend there is something greater in Germany than the Nazi inspiration. They deny that the *Führer is* Germany. The excuse they offer for turning traitor is that the *Führer* has repeatedly rejected their advice to retreat and save the Army from the disaster they fear. They want to crawl to the Allies, make a shameful peace, break our people's morale, convince them that the war is lost!"

The Commandant's voice cracked, and something near to madness looked out of eyes that were usually so lacking in expression.

Erich flinched before the fanaticism of this man. And in spite of his training, in spite of his years of hitherto unquestioning devotion to the Nazi cause, at that moment a doubt crept into his mind. Was his country on the verge of disaster? Could it be true that the *Führer* was going out of his mind? . . . The rumor of his madness was rife in Paris.

The Commandant was speaking again, his voice reduced to its normal tone. "You have heard what our *Führer* has said: his new secret weapons will bring the British to their knees, reduce their war effort to chaos!" He indicated the preparations going on around them, the empty filing cabinets and stacks of papers. "All this is quite unnecessary. The Allies will never reach Paris!"

Yes, Erich thought wearily, I know all about those secret weapons; who could escape knowing, with the Propaganda Department flooding the radio with assurances of the havoc being wrought in southern England?

A week after D-Day, Hitler had announced that guided missiles were being directed to England from launching sites in the French Channel ports. These missiles had struck terror into the British. They called them "doodle-bugs"—"buzz bombs," Erich had heard. The British were like that—they would not give a thing of terror a terrifying name. He could imagine that terror: the engine of the missile droning overhead, then suddenly cutting out. A moment of silence: then the explosion, equivalent to that of a one-ton bomb. There were other missiles which would soon be in use, too: highspeed rockets traveling faster than sound, to be launched from bases in Holland into the heart of London. There would be no warning of their arrival: the high-pitched whine of their passage through the air would follow the explosion. . . .

But still Erich could not shake off that nagging doubt. In spite of the secret weapons—the doodlebugs—the British were *not* beaten to their knees. In fact, they were uncomfortably near Paris. . . . And in spite of the Commandant's remarks about the Officer Korps, Rommel had been a hero.

The Commandant brought the interview to a close. "I know I can rely on the complete loyalty of each member of my staff," he said. (Did he say that to reassure himself?) "Heil Hitler!"

"Heil Hitler!" Erich responded, giving lip service to the swastika he wore upon his sleeve.

As the Allies approached Paris, French underground fighters engaged the enemy in hand-to-hand battles in the streets. American and Free French forces surrounded the city; and on August 25, General de Gaulle and General Leclerc, leaders of the Free French Army, marched down the Champs-Élysées amid delirious rejoicing. That day, the liberation of Paris was celebrated in Notre Dame Cathedral.

Clothilde Duchesne sat down to write a letter to England, the first for four years.

"Dearest Suzanne, my beloved niece, I am writing this on the great day of liberation. Outside, the crowds are

cheering and singing in the streets. Every shop window
is decorated with the Tricolor, the Stars and Stripes, and
the Union Jack. De Gaulle is the hero of the hour—de
Gaulle and the Americans, who, as they drive through
the city in their jeeps and tanks, are besieged by all the
pretty girls in Paris!

"But there are others who are not so happy today—the
collaborateurs, those who worked with the Boche and
helped to bring death to our Resistance fighters . . ."

She stopped writing for a moment, and glanced towards the frayed muslin curtain at the open window of
her apartment. That morning, she had heard a dreadful
screaming from the pavement below. A man known for
his Nazi sympathies had been hunted and discovered.
She shivered, and went on:

"Those foolish women, too, who were the girl friends
of the German officers, are being punished for the favors
they dispensed. They are seized in the streets and have
their hair cropped with razors so that everyone will know
them.

"My dear Suzanne, had you known Paris during this
dreadful occupation, you would have wept for her. But
now her youth returns, and there will be color once more.

"I have no news of your Cousin Raoul. All I know is
that he was with the Free French Forces, I believe in
Africa. Hourly I pray for his return. As for myself, I am
a little older, but I have managed to live despite some
privations. I long to see you again, and your dear father.
Write soon, and tell me how it has gone with you. I await
your news with eager impatience. Your loving Aunt
Clothilde."

She reached for an envelope and wrote out the address: Mlle. Suzanne Sinclair, 11 St. Oswald's Terrace, Renchester, Angleterre.

Then she went over to a cupboard and produced a carefully hoarded tin of coffee. Real coffee, extravagantly bought on the black market, and saved for such a day as this. Now for the coffeepot and a match for the stove . . .

As she went into the kitchen, the doorbell rang. That ring! A long buzz, then four short, two long . . . Only one person ever rang her doorbell like that. Her heart beating wildly, her mouth trembling, she opened the door to welcome home her son.

While the Americans, led by General Bradley, turned towards Paris, Field-Marshal Montgomery led the British 21st Army Group north from Normandy. They overran the flying-bomb sites, capturing Le Havre, Calais, Boulogne, and Dunkirk. Brussels fell on September 3, Antwerp the next day. The Allied armies advanced to the banks of the Rhine. Belgium and Luxemburg were liberated.

During that summer of 1944, people in Britain told each other: "It'll all be over this year." "Germany will collapse by December." "Hitler is at the end of the road." They were wrong, for though victory might now be certain, still the war held shocks and setbacks for the Allies as well as advances and success.

The Golem, the Golem, the Golem

A sergeants' mess somewhere in northern France. Geoff
Chanter and Chalky White were sharing a table, drinking beer and reading out-of-date newspapers. Orders had
just come through that their division was to go to the
Ardennes, where the United States First Army had been
thrown back by panzer troops launching a final desperate
offensive. The Germans had advanced several miles into
Belgium and Luxemburg and had succeeded in driving a
wedge between the American lines. Now General Pat-
ton's American troops from the south, and British forces
from the north, were speeding to plug the gap. This was
the Battle of the Bulge.

It was December. Outside, the sky was yellow, heavy
with unfallen snow.

Chalky White turned the pages of the *Daily Mirror*.
"Official stand-down of Home Guard: King takes salute

in Hyde Park," he read out. "You know something? We
joined the wrong army. I'd rather be marching along
Rotten Row than off to the Ardennes, I can tell you!"

Geoff grinned. "Cheer up, Chalky, we'll both be marching in Hyde Park one day, I expect—in the veterans'
parade. Can't you see us? Best suits, medals clinking, and
the kids calling out, 'Look at those poor old men!' "

Chalky grunted, looked at the Jane cartoon, then concentrated on a piece called "Where Is Hitler?" According to this article, the *Führer* now spent his days in a
concrete bunker under his Chancellery in Berlin.

Geoff looked into his beer glass. He shared Chalky's
gloom. Fighting in winter was so much worse than fighting in summer. Frozen fingers and bulky clothing ham-
pered action: mist and rain blurred your vision. It
certainly looked as though they were in for a packet where
they were going, too. Still, this must be the final phase,
the enemy's last struggle with his back to the wall. Well,
the Jerries just couldn't go on much longer. Why on
earth didn't they admit they'd bought it? The Fifth and
Eighth Armies were storming their defenses in the
Apennines, after capturing Rome and Florence; part of
the Red Army was through Finland and into Norway,
while the rest of the Russians advanced on Vienna. . . .
It seemed as though the Russians might be first into Berlin, the way things were going—and maybe that wasn't
so good. It didn't seem as though you could trust those
Commies. Look at the way Stalin had behaved over the
liberation of Warsaw.

Geoff's thoughts went back five months. When the advancing Russian troops were only ten miles from War-

saw, the Polish underground army had risen against their Nazi oppressors in the city. The Germans had rushed in troops to suppress the rising—and the Russian advance had been halted. Stalin refused to drop supplies by air to the Polish fighters; nor would he allow British and American aircraft to do so; he refused permission for them to use Soviet airfields. The half-armed Poles held out for sixty-three days. British and American planes made one attempt to take them supplies, flying from their remote airbases—but it was too late. The Germans succeeded in completely suppressing the rising, and when the Russians finally entered Warsaw, the city was devastated. Stalin had shown that he would not allow Poland to be set free by anyone except the Communists. He showed no mercy, no sympathy for the Poles who had fought so desperately. All human feelings were sacrificed before the cause of Communism.

Well—whoever reached Berlin first, it was only a question of time now. But meanwhile—Geoff Chanter and Chalky White, and a few thousand others (among them a G.I. called Spike Rodgers) must fight the Battle of the Bulge. Those were the orders of the day.

Ah, well, with luck, this time next year, Geoff thought, he'd be back at his desk. How were things at Stanford & Earle? he wondered. That girl with the sharp tongue —Marion. She was probably married by now—if she'd found anyone brave enough to take her on! A composite recollection of smells: fish-paste sandwich crumbs, carbon paper, scented ink, seemed to fill his nostrils. . . .

"Reading the crystal ball?" Chalky's voice broke into his reverie.

Geoff raised his glass and drained it. "That's it," he said, "I can see a perishing snowstorm in the Ardennes forests, and a dark stranger with a swastika on his arm."

It was March, 1945, when Montgomery's armies crossed the Rhine just north of the Ruhr and set foot on German soil. The Allies were closing in on Germany from three sides. The northern armies joined General Bradley's forces, who had crossed the Rhine at Remagen. The entire Ruhr garrison, stronghold of Germany's industry, surrendered on April 18.

In this hour of triumph, the death of Franklin D. Roosevelt was announced. He had been elected to a third term of office as President of the United States only the preceding November. Now the world was without the wisdom and guidance he could have brought to the peacemakers.

As the Allied Forces went on through Germany, they found the dreaded concentration camps: Dachau, Belsen, and Buchenwald, where terrible scenes of disease and torture and death were revealed.

Gordon Pearce was one member of a medical team sent from Britain soon after Dachau was liberated, to do whatever could be done to relieve the rampant tuberculosis, dysentery, typhus—and starvation. As he entered the camp, he recoiled from the scene before his eyes. Piles of dead and dying children were swept together like flies that have been trapped in a shuttered room. Creatures of skin and bone clawed each other aside to reach the food their liberators offered. The long-term captives were reduced to a horrible similarity: it was impossible to tell, merely by regarding their sunken eyes and shrunken bodies, whether they were old or young. The stench of death and decay was everywhere, especially around the gas chambers and the incinerators where bodies had been stacked for burning. The whole camp was an obscene nightmare monstrously turned into reality in broad daylight.

Gordon was shaken by horror in a place where horror had become a commonplace. He thought of Esmé, his wife, who was now awaiting the birth of their first baby. He thought of the loving concern they had both already given to their unborn child—and then he looked again at the disregarded children who had died here by the hundreds, who had been pushed over the edge of civilization into a state of being where a human became a four-limbed animal.

From somewhere far away, beyond the world, he seemed to hear Suzanne's voice saying: ". . . bombs—invasion—the Nazi concentration camps . . . have men and women ever faced such horrors as these?" She had not said children, though; it was the fate of the children that was the most horrifying thing of all.

In the camp hospital, another doctor attended a man in the last stages of tuberculosis. He was probably young, and the interpreter said he spoke Czechoslovakian.

"What is he saying? Can we discover who he is?" The doctor stopped; it was hopeless to attempt to identify each of these dying victims.

The interpreter shrugged. "He does not speak sense. He imagines there is some evil thing which pursues him always. He keeps calling it by a name: he says it is the —Golem. He must take a paper from its mouth. . . . Now he is calling its name again: the Golem, the Golem, the

Golem . . . but all this is nonsense, Doctor. He is out of his mind."

The doctor looked at the man's wasted face and glittering eyes, then passed on. There was no time to waste on a madman's ravings.

A few days later, Tomas Jelinck died, not even knowing that the prison camp had been liberated.

Now the Russian forces swept into Germany from Vienna and joined the northern and western Allied armies. At the end of April, Berlin was encircled. Hitler, still in his concrete bunker under the garden of the Chancellery, shot himself. Goebbels followed his example. Other Nazi leaders escaped from Berlin; later, most of them were captured and brought to trial for their war crimes before the International Court at Nuremberg.

On May 7, 1945, the German commander in chief signed an unconditional surrender to the representatives of the United States, Britain, France, and Russia.

The war in Europe was over.

Thanksgiving for victory in the churches: in London, on V-E Day, processions, and a vast crowd cheering outside Buckingham Palace. The Royal Family acknowledging the cheers, waving from the palace balcony, with Princess Elizabeth in her ATS uniform.

And in Renchester, as in a thousand other towns and suburbs and villages, there were celebrations in the streets. Blackout was thrown aside. Light streamed from uncurtained windows and open doorways; car headlamps were unmasked; bonfires and beacons blazed from hilltops. In Povey Street, they danced to the music of someone's accordion—the Lambeth Walk, the Hokey-Cokey, Boomps-a-Daisy, with laughter and gaiety that lasted until the small hours.

Up on the Sandilands Estate, in Derwent Crescent, someone was throwing a party: car doors slammed as more guests arrived, loud voices were raised in greeting, radio dance music blared through an open window.

At number seven, the Jelincks celebrated quietly.

Loud singing came from the house where the party was in full swing—

> *I'm going to get lit up*
> *When the lights go up in London,*
> *Lit up as I've never been before . . .*

Anna helped her mother with the supper dishes, and in the midst of this homely task, she suddenly came out with the secret hope she had nourished for years.

"Mother, do you think that Tomas . . . that he might be still alive?"

Though Anna herself could have told the answer as well as her mother, nevertheless she asked the question—as an infant asks questions of its parents, never doubting their omniscience.

"Oh, my Anna!" Her mother's hands, cobwebbed with soapsuds, were stretched towards her in a loving, hopeless gesture. "Long ago, I stop dreaming that might be true. I tell myself, 'He is gone from us. Never will we see him again.' No, my Anna, it is best that you should stop hoping too."

The newsreel pictures of the concentration camps were fresh in Anna's mind; they had been shown at the Eldorado. That was what she and her parents had escaped from. Had it been Tomas's fate? In a book of English poems, she had read some verses written during the First World War, called "The War Films"—

> *Brother of men, when now I see*
> *The lads go forth in line,*
> *. . . Thou knowest my heart is bowed in me*
> *To take their death for mine.*

Anna felt profoundly humble. She had been spared; so many, many other things had perished.

Antonia Jelinck looked at her daughter's downcast head. "I hope for something else that concerns your father. . . ." She lowered her voice; Josef was in the next room, talking to old Mr. Seton, and as yet she had not disclosed her plan to him.

"What, Mother? What is it?"

"When first we come in England," her mother said softly, "I think your father should seek to have his arm made better. So we see a doctor. He tells us an operation is necessary to bring the nerves back to life. But that would cost much money, and we have no money. But now Lady Cortley, when last she comes to see me, has told me of this new plan, that soon all peoples in England shall pay a little money each week to the Government, and when we are in illness or need to stay in hospital, there will not have a great sum of money to be found all at the same time. And so I think—now, perhaps, my Josef can find out more about this operation. Perhaps—perhaps he may once again the violin to play!"

"Oh, Mother, how wonderful that would be!" This

new idea took root in Anna's mind, pushing aside her old, childish dream that Tomas would come back.

Her mother watched her, smiling gently. "We must persuade your father to visit with the doctors again, my Anna."

Mary, the Land Girl, and Angelo, the Italian ex-POW, walked up a country lane, arms entwined around each other's waists. The sickly sweet scents of cow parsley and may blossom wafted from the hedges. A beacon blazed on a hilltop to the west: the villagers were dancing round the flames, singing songs, celebrating the Allies' victory just as long ago an earlier race of men had celebrated the yearly victory of the sun god on the selfsame hilltop. A bull, disturbed by the noise and the flames, bellowed in his field.

Angelo had said he would marry Mary; but first he was going back to Italy to see his family. Mary wondered if he would come back as he'd promised. If he didn't— well, there were plenty of boys coming home to England now. And, sometimes, Angelo did go off the deep end a bit. He got so excited about things, not like an English boy. Look at the way he'd gone on when he saw the newspaper photograph of Mussolini after the Italian partisans had killed him and strung up his body in public.

"*Il Duce! Il Duce!*" he'd sobbed. "Look at him! But look! We thought he was a god!"

It had been shocking, really. Perhaps, Mary thought, it would be best if he stayed in Italy and forgot all about her. . . .

October that year brought an early winter. One gusty day, Marion was working at her desk when a sudden draft blew a sheaf of papers to the floor.

"Shut the door, can't you!" she cried irritably, not looking up, assuming it was the office boy bringing her afternoon cup of tea.

"Certainly, *ma'am*," replied a mocking voice.

She looked up then. "Oh—it's you!"

Geoff Chanter stood there in his brand-new demobilization suit. Marion stared at him. The rather weedy, pale-faced clerk who had gone off to war four years ago had somehow enlarged into a self-assured man with a weatherbeaten complexion.

Geoff grinned at her. "Don't bother to tell me how glad you are to see me. I'll take it for granted."

Marion fidgeted with her pen. "Well, Geoff . . . er— have you seen Mr. Stanford yet?"

She was eager to know what would be the result of that interview.

"Yes. It's back at the grindstone for me from Monday next. I'm to have Mr. Earle's old office."

"Mr. Earle's office!" Marion sounded as put out by this piece of news as she felt. She'd been hoping to move in there herself; it was high time she had something better to work in than her present cubbyhole.

"Mr. Stanford said he hoped we'd work together well, you and I," Geoff continued. "I—er—gather you've taken on a good bit of extra work since we last saw each other. The boss told me all about your exam successes. Congratulations! I'll have to catch up on all that."

"Yes," said Marion bitterly, "I've no doubt you will."

This was the reward of her hard work and devotion

to duty! To be cast on one side as soon as the conquering hero returned! Phrases of self-pity came readily to her mind.

"So Mr. Stanford hoped we'd work together well, did he?" she repeated in an ominous tone. This, she thought, was where she made her decision: she'd find out about jobs in London straight away, leave Renchester as soon as she could. . . .

"We'll have our hands full the next few months, I expect," Geoff went on, wondering if Marion was permanently bad-tempered these days, or whether he had just caught her in a bad mood. "I see there are prefabs going up outside the town: homes fit for heroes!"

"Yes, there're plenty of people wanting places to live just now—mostly chaps like you, just demobbed." Last week, she had managed to interest one of them in her parents' house in Povey Street; her father was buying a bungalow on the Sandilands Estate as she'd hoped he would.

Someone else had come into the office that very morning, inquiring for a house—someone Marion had recognized, though he hadn't seemed to know her. Tony Welsh, the boy whose face she'd slapped at the Mawtons' housewarming party, years ago! He'd come in with his fiancée, a tall girl with shining blonde hair, carelessly wearing a beautiful camel-hair coat. They'd asked for Mr. Stanford, but he was busy, so Marion had given them the particulars of several properties. "I'll let Mr. Stanford know if any of these interest us," Tony Welsh had said—and Marion had felt like a parlormaid who has been given a visiting card by a caller because the mistress of the house was not at home.

"What's this I hear about the boss's daughter marrying a Yank?" Geoff said. "I never thought *she'd* end up as a G.I. bride!"

"Well, she has," Marion replied shortly. "Geoff, I'm rather busy now, if you don't mind——"

He saw it was no use hoping for a friendly chat. He'd come prepared to take Marion out for a drink, too, just to talk over old times . . . with anyone else, it could have been fun. He decided to go along to the Crooked Billet on his own; there was sure to be some one there he'd know.

"See you Monday," he said, picking up his demob. hat.

"And shut the door after you," Marion replied as he went out of the room.